Because I Had To

Because I Had To

David Bulitt

Winchester, UK
Washington, USA

First published by Roundfire Books, 2017
Roundfire Books is an imprint of John Hunt Publishing Ltd., Laurel House, Station Approach,
Alresford, Hants, SO24 9JH, UK
office1@jhpbooks.net
www.johnhuntpublishing.com
www.roundfire-books.com

For distributor details and how to order please visit the 'Ordering' section on our website.

Text copyright: David Bulitt 2016

ISBN: 978 1 78535 551 6
978 1 78535 552 3 (ebook)
Library of Congress Control Number: 2016944524

A CIP catalogue record for this book is available from the British Library.

Design: Stuart Davies

Printed and bound by CPI Group (UK) Ltd, Croydon, CR0 4YY, UK

We operate a distinctive and ethical publishing philosophy in all
areas of our business, from our global network of authors to
production and worldwide distribution.

ONE

Jess

It does feel good. The bathroom is the only place in this little shit box that I really like, so maybe that's why I spent my entire decorating allowance in here. "Decorating allowance?" That is funny. I sound a little bit like my mom when I say it just so, turning my nose a certain way and fluttering my eyelids. My mom, who never thought I was good enough for—well, just about anything—she and I haven't talked in almost a year. When I left, I took some of the money that my dad had left me after he died, and with the rest saved from work, that was all I needed for a security deposit and one month's rent on this, my palace, a first-floor apartment in Jones Beach, Florida, a good thousand miles away from where I grew up. After my dad died, I thought about going west, to California or Arizona maybe, but instead I followed my friend Macy down here because she got me a job.

When we were little, my dad used to repeat the line from a movie we used to watch and tell both my sister and me that "all girls are princesses." Well, it hasn't exactly worked out that way, but once in a while, I still try to think of myself as a princess, so I call this place my palace. Just to myself, though.

The water in the tub is just the right temperature. Thankfully, tonight the pressure is high enough; some days, I barely can get any hot water much less enough to fill my tub. I have my legs hiked up on either side of the faucet, and I've slid down to just the right angle so the water is pounding right where it needs to go. The tub is a little small, like the one I had in my old house when I shared a bathroom with my sister. Instead of yellow, this one is a commercial greenie kind of color. Or maybe it's blue. It's hard to tell. Not that it matters at this particular moment.

The stopper on the tub broke after I moved in, so I had to buy a rubber one from Rite Aid. It fits in the drain pretty well, but

1

sometimes it pops out and unless I can jam it in real quick, all the water runs out and I have to start refilling again. That gets particularly annoying, especially if I am in the middle of the "bathtub trick" as I like to call it when I get off in here. The stopper is in there nice and tight right now, and with the level low and the water running hard, all systems look to be a go.

When I have been with a boy, it is good too. I like having him touch me, rubbing me on just the right spot, getting inside of me, sliding in and out. But somehow, when I am with someone else, it's different. Like when I was little trying to climb the big hill in the Thompson's yard, it takes a while. That hill was a mountain to a ten-year-old girl. I have to get up slowly and pay attention to other things while I am working my way up before I can turn and enjoy the race back down. When I am in the tub, with the water running between my legs, pounding and throbbing, there is no climb. It's a quick pump up the mountain and then down I go over the slippery side, breathing hard, racing as fast as I can, like riding on greased-up skis, catching the wind and hitting a stride, coming in a matter of seconds.

My mind wanders as it often does just before focusing on what is going on below my waist. As soon as I rented this place, the first thing I did was run over to Pottery Barn in the mall and buy a distressed wooden ladder shelf that now sits in the corner, holding a Votivo vanilla-scented candle and Warm Vanilla Sugar lotion and body spray. When I was a little girl, I loved vanilla ice cream; it was the only flavor I would eat. I don't eat ice cream as much as I used to, probably because it reminds me too much of my dad, but I get my vanilla fix now from my candles, body sprays, and gels. I also have a set of really soft bright pink towels resting on the bottom ledge of the ladder. They were expensive—the HOTEL COLLECTION from Macy's—but every time I get out of the tub and wrap myself in one I sure am glad I bought them.

I can feel myself starting to tighten inside and as if a lead singer just counted down a song introduction—"*a one, two, three, four*"—and is starting to sing my hips are rocking up and down under the faucet. For a second, I think how funny it would look if someone came in and saw me humping the flow of tap water. But the second passes quickly and now I am focusing more on me. I can feel my breathing quicken. I feel hot, and my face is beading with just the slightest bit of sweat. I touch my nipple, swollen and hard, with my left hand, continuing to hold on to the faucet with my right so I don't slip under and inadvertently drown myself. I reach down from my breast and try to put my finger inside myself, just enough so I can feel it, but without upsetting the water rushing to my clitoris. The water is getting higher, not yet to *Titanic* levels, so I have a minute or so to finish. I can't quite reach in as far as I would like, and at this moment, I really wish my arms were a little longer or I had "the fingers of a piano player" like my sister. I feel the rush coming and tip my head back, resting lightly on the opposite side of the tub.

For some reason, just as my teeth clench and my back arches, my ADHD kicks in and I notice the rusty stain on the ceiling above me from when my friend Bobby in the apartment upstairs overflowed his shower and part of the drywall plopped right into my tub while I was brushing my teeth, maybe three days after I moved in. Bobby, who works two jobs as the super for the building and manager of the bar where I work, said he fixed it, but from the signs of the steadily spreading stain above me, he might need to come back and take another look. I almost laugh, thinking of asking Bobby down to see the stain, but can't because I am holding my breath and before I know it, the pulsing starts, I'm biting my lip and pulling that flow of water onto me, into me. I am flying down that mountain.

After I get my breath back, I swing my legs back around and slide down into the tub, the way it was designed to be used.

I remember reading in *Women's Health* or *Cosmo* or one of those types of magazines that the best way to make sure a woman has an orgasm is for her to have a steamy shower, a lot of foreplay, and maybe some oral sex first. Not me. Especially when I do the bathtub trick, I'm like a thirteen-year-old boy who just discovered his dick. A couple of minutes under the running water and pow—I'm good to go.

I get out of the tub and reach for my HOTEL COLLECTION towel. The orgasm felt good. Great even. But fuck, it just sucks. I'm not satisfied.

I need more.

I need to cut.

I start rummaging through my medicine cabinet, pushing aside a jar of Burt's Bees eye cream and the bottles of medications I have been prescribed over the last year. I haven't done it in a while, but I know I bought those blades a few months ago. The ones other people use to remove calluses on their feet. They're perfect, yes, but I don't see them.

Goddamn it, I need to find them. I bend down and my towel falls onto the cracked tile floor as I start to rummage through the cabinet under the sink. I immediately see the packaging— "Tweezerman" blades—they are made in Germany and come twenty in a pack. Hair thin and crazy sharp, they make the most amazing cut. Only one blade is missing from the pack; I used it a few months ago and tossed it away after, promising that would be the last time. At the time, I heard the ringing voice of my therapist in my ear. *"It's unacceptable, Jess. It's just a negative coping mechanism. You need to find positive ways to cope with things."*

Fuck her and her positive things. I need to do it. Now.

There really isn't anything else that makes me feel as good. Not running, which I took up after my dad died, not working at the bar, not even the bathtub trick. Nothing else makes me feel as good, gives me that same high.

I remember exactly when I first tried it. After school one day, I came home on the bus with my sister and a few of her friends. I didn't have any of my own friends, so I tried to glom on to hers.

When one of the girls, Bonnie I think her name was, told my sister to "tell the weirdo to get out of here," I left the kitchen, pretending not to care, and went upstairs to my room. I plopped onto my bed and tried to do some homework, fiddling with a shiny paper clip between my fingers.

I was angry, as usual. Angry at myself. Angry at my sister. Angry at my parents. Angry. Why didn't my friends come over after school? I was always up here, by myself, either because I did something wrong and got sent here or because I just had no place else to go.

Although I always blamed everyone else, I knew that there must be something wrong with me. I wasn't good enough to sit still and watch TV with my parents, like my sister did. There had to be a reason that people didn't like me. I should be punished, I thought.

I opened up the paper clip and made a short scratch inside my forearm. I liked it. I scratched a bit more and kept going until I had carved a short line up the inside of my forearm and into my elbow. It bled a little bit and I watched the bright red streak meander toward my palm. Later, when my dad noticed the scratch and asked me what happened, I just told him that I had an accident with some scissors while I was doing a school project.

I pulled one of the thin blades from the pack and rolled my arm over onto the countertop. I looked at myself naked in the mirror, hair still wet and tangled across my forehead. My body is as good as it will ever look, I thought. My breasts are round and firm and high; Bobby says they could "hold a coke can on top" but I haven't tried to see if that's true. I have curves that I used to hate when I was younger and obsessively comparing myself to all the skinny, athlete types but now appreciate. I look okay. After this though, I will be back to wearing long sleeves again. It doesn't matter. It just feels good. In this moment, nothing else matters.

3

I need that release.
I want that feeling.
I cut.

TWO

Jess

My dad is dead. It's been almost a year now. He was pretty young, only fifty-two. When I think back on all I have done since I last saw him, I'm not sure how I should feel. Embarrassed? Some, yes. But also proud of myself, in a strange sort of way. At twenty-three, I've probably done more than a lot of people have. Or should have, anyway.

I made it at home for just a little while after he died. Me, my mom, and my sister. And that's exactly how it was. Me. My mom and my sister.

Kasey and I are twins. We were born in Pittsburgh and adopted right away. My parents did not use an agency but got us through what they always told us was an independent adoption. They found us by running some sort of "baby wanted" ads in local papers and those penny saver things that people look at in grocery stores.

Ever since I can remember, Kasey and I were different. As twins, one would think that we would have a connection, a natural bond of some kind, permanent "womb-mates." For whatever reason, though, I never felt it. More than that, I never even liked Kasey. I know it's crazy to say, but as far back as when I was about six or so, I can remember wishing that something bad would happen to her. Of course, for a little kid, "something bad" usually meant like her hair falling out or hoping she threw up all over herself. Once when we were little and on the couch exploring the depths of our prepubescent vaginas while watching *SpongeBob* and playing that stupid "Pretty Pretty Princess" game my sister loved so much, I handed Kasey a clip-on earring and told her to put it on that little bump thing just above her vagina.

"It will tickle."

I lied.

7

Like the mindless sheep she was, Kasey immediately snapped it right on to her clitoris. She went screaming through the house and it wasn't until my dad could catch her and was able to pry her legs apart long enough to unhook the thing that she finally quieted down. I didn't exactly know what a clitoris was at the time, but it sure looked like it hurt. I stayed on the couch and laughed my ass off.

As we got older, I stopped wishing for Kasey to take a fall somewhere along the manicured little path that my mother paved for her. Like old bathroom wallpaper that no one notices, I just stopped thinking about her altogether.

Same as my mom, Kasey always seemed perfect. When we were kids, her hair was long and light brown and curly. She had this creamy translucent white skin and I don't think has ever, even now, gotten a pimple. She reminded me of one of those irritating American Girl dolls. When we would brush our teeth together in the banana-yellow double-sink bathroom that we shared, I always looked over at her in one of her little pink Lanz nightgowns, buttoned up all the way to the top. When she finished, Kasey would rinse out the toothbrush and put it right back into the holder, exactly where it belonged. I looked at her, and then straight ahead into the mirror at myself, toothpaste running down my chin.

My hair was a bit darker and much straighter than my sister's. I had this awful freckle on the tip of my nose that to me looked like a little licorice jellybean. I picked it off over and over again, must have been a hundred times, only to have it always grow right back. The summer before I went to high school, my dad took me to a plastic surgeon who took it off with a laser.

I did everything I could to get my hair to curl like Kasey's. I tried my mom's curling iron, burning my fingers more times than I care to remember. A few times, I tried tying my dad's socks into it overnight, hoping to wake up and see one of those unrealistically cute Disney channel characters in the mirror. One time, I had my dad drive me to a dollar store and bought my own set of 1950s-style curlers. I put them in and one became so tangled that the next morning my dad had to cut it out, leaving a short, jagged patch. Nothing worked. When I got a little older, I just gave up, and instead, just let my bangs grow and brushed them over to the side and across my forehead, often low enough to cover my left eye. My hair-never-out-of-place mother didn't approve. More than once, she told me that I looked like one of the Beach Boys. I didn't know who they were back then, but I knew she did not mean it to be a compliment. I asked my dad to play me some of their music and thought it was pretty good. After that, I didn't really mind the comparison.

Like everything else we owned, my mom bought us the same nightgowns. I hated those things, all frilly and soft. Kasey kept hers folded tightly in her "nightgown drawer." I just never felt comfortable in them and stuffed them into little balls underneath my bed. Instead, I would rummage through my dad's old T-shirt drawer and steal one of his particularly big and baggy ones. It drove my mother crazy, but Dad kind of liked it. Even now, at 23, I still wear his old T-shirts. Except for his Asbury Jukes music collection, what's left in my bank account, and some great fucking memories, those old T-shirts are pretty much all I have left of him.

THREE

Jess

I can't really say where my distaste—that's a good word—my *distaste* for Kasey came from. Maybe it was because of how differently our parents treated us. Actually, that's not fair. My mom treated us differently. The first time I can remember knowing that there was a difference between Kasey and me was at our sixth birthday party. I wanted to have a party in our yard, with games and squirt guns and treasure hunts and piñatas. Instead, as usual, my mom got us what Kasey wanted. We had one of those lame little girl parties where some otherwise unemployed misfit dressed up as Jasmine from the *Aladdin* cartoon movie showed up and helped all the girls with their hair and makeup. Kasey was happy as a fucking clam, sitting with all of her boring and perfect little friends getting their nails done. Of course, my mom was right next to Kasey the entire time, laughing and smiling, like some big puffed-up six-year-old princess wannabe. All the while, my dad roamed around with one of those old-style video cameras making home movies that no one ever wants to watch.

I spent most of the afternoon brooding, eating cake and sitting by myself. In one of my early exhibitions of what would later be diagnosed as oppositional defiant disorder, I refused to invite any of my friends to the crappy party. Not that I had many friends.

At some point as the festivities came to an end, I was able to lure one of Kasey's better friends, Christine, out to our shed in the back of the yard. All of Kasey's friends thought I was weird and I am sure that some of their parents told them to stay away from me. Christine was a bit of a dope, though, and when I whispered to her about the Aladdin carpet in our garage, she padded into the shed behind me like a golden retriever puppy.

Some things you can't forget.

"It's over there in the corner. Aladdin's carpet."

"Really? Where? I want to see it and take it to Jasmine so she and I can go for a ride!"

Dummy.

"Keep walking. It's pink and purple." Couldn't help myself.

She kept looking. "Where? I don't see it."

"Over there past the lawn mower thing."

Christine did her best to find that carpet in the shed that was barely lit with just a little sunshine poking through the metal roof.

"Oh, yeah. There it is. Yay!"

She was so excited that for a second I can remember thinking well, maybe there is a magic carpet.

Nah.

I scampered out of the shed, slammed the door shut, and locked it.

When Christine's mom showed up to take her home, all hell broke loose. No one knew where she was; my parents scurried around the house, inside and out. I waited a few minutes, then snuck back to the shed and opened the door. Guess she couldn't take a joke.

The little shit had pissed her pants and immediately told everyone that I was the culprit.

Got me a good spanking for that one.

Later that night, I pulled my blankets off and sat up in bed. I had a lot of trouble sleeping in those days. I could hear my parents talking from their room down the hall. They weren't exactly arguing, but they didn't seem too happy either.

"Why are they so different?" I had heard my mom ask this question before.

"I don't know. It's who she is. Jess is not Kasey. You need to find a way to connect with her, too," my dad said.

"I just can't. I mean, I do love her. I guess. I just don't like her. Sometimes I even hate her, really."

I knew that. The hate part.

"Don't ever say that. Jesus Christ, Lianne. She is a kid. She's not the only one who gets into trouble. No one guaranteed that everything would be perfect when we decided to have kids. You need to find some way. Go back to therapy. Something." My dad sounded like he was begging.

"I just don't understand. Why does she act the way she does? Why does she have to do those things?"

"I don't know, Lianne. I really don't know," my dad said.

I don't know either, I thought.

I stuck my head back under the covers.

FOUR

JB

"Overruled" was Judge McDonough's response.

Really? I thought to myself. This dolt in a robe had just allowed a newspaper article into evidence during the second day of my latest divorce trial.

Everyone I know has a TV and most people have watched some sort of lawyer program that involved an unrealistic and overdramatized courtroom scene. Those scenes almost always include an objection from one of the actor-lawyers, followed by something like *"it's hearsay, your honor."* The actor-judge, looking steely and stern, pauses and then responds by declaring, *"sustained."* Sometimes he even bangs his gavel.

For the most part, the hearsay rule is pretty simple. In lawyer-speak, "hearsay" is a statement made by someone else being offered during a trial to prove its truth. So, if during a particularly dimwitted episode of *Law and Order*, Smitty, the accomplice, tries to testify that his partner, Jake, said to him, "I'm going to kill that motherfucker next Tuesday," that would be hearsay, as would a note written by Smitty's friend telling him that the dastardly Jake was planning to do the killing.

To be bare bones about it, generally speaking, a witness cannot testify about what someone else said or wrote. That is, of course, unless the so-called statement falls within one of the many exceptions to the rule. If that sounds a little like parenting, that's because it is. We all have rules for our kids that we bend and often break, sometimes because we want to, but often because it's just easier not to enforce a rule. Same with the hearsay rule. It's human nature to want to know what someone else said and sharp lawyers know just that. If a lawyer can find a way around the hearsay rule by convincing a judge that the statement, whether written or spoken, falls within one of the "exceptions," into evidence it goes.

One of the dozen or so exceptions to the hearsay rule is called the "business entries exception." This exception allows documents kept in the ordinary course of business to be admitted into evidence under the general theory that there is some circumstantial guarantee of trustworthiness in a document that employees habitually prepare and save. There is a certain logic to the exception with which I don't take issue—certainly many reports and documents kept by a business, such as receipts, daily timesheets, sales reports, and the like, should be admissible at a trial without the necessity of calling the actual individual who prepared those reports to testify about their content.

A newspaper article, however, to any rational or logical person—not to mention someone entrusted with actually knowing the law—does not qualify as a business record. So, when the astute Judge McDonough allowed an article from the *Style* section of the *Washington Post* headlined "The Price of Tea on K Street" as evidence that my client, the owner of a couple of local coffeehouses, was enjoying skyrocketing profits and could therefore afford a significantly higher alimony payment, my head almost exploded.

"Respectfully, Judge, it's an article from a newspaper."

This guy deserved anything but respect, but, as a lawyer, it seems that I must have spoken or written the word "respectfully" about a billion times. This guy was plucking my nerves, though, and I couldn't help myself.

"It's not a record of anything other than what was in the newspaper that morning," I said. "And this article by Walter whatever-his-name-is cannot in any way be offered as evidence to as to what my client is earning. I mean, this is first-year law school stuff."

Shit. That last crack might have gone a bit too far, I thought.

"Respectfully," I added.

"Respectfully," he said, leaning forward in his chair. "Your objection is overruled. Take it up on appeal if you like, counsel," Judge McDonough said, knowing my client had neither the inclination nor the resources to ask an appellate court to tell him what the rest of us in the courtroom already knew—that he was wrong.

Had this happened twenty-five years ago when I was just cutting my teeth in this business and still thought that judges were smarter than the rest of us, I would have probably answered simply, "Yes, sir," and sat back down without as much as a whimper. Now, though, having dealt with more than my share of these self-impressed characters, I sighed, rolled my eyes, shook my head, and spun away from the judge, moving back toward my chair at the trial table.

Clearly recognizing the disrespect I was directing his way, Judge McDonough was not happy and called my attention to some contempt of his own. "Don't turn your back on me in my courtroom, counsel," he bellowed. "Do it again, I'll find you in contempt. We have places here in the courthouse where you can sit and think for a while if you wish."

I looked to my left and noticed a young glassy-eyed deputy fiddling with his handcuffs, looking anxious to do something other than sit in the back of the courtroom, gnaw on his cuticles, and doze. Realizing that this protest of mine was going to get my client nowhere and me "thinking for a while" in a jail cell downstairs, I turned back around, and in my best good boy voice, said, "My apologies, Your Honor. It won't happen again."

Judge McDonough banged his gavel, shot me a major "don't fuck with me" glare, and called for a recess until the next morning.

FIVE

JB

One of my best friends, Tom Porter, died just about a year ago. He was my age, not much over fifty at the time. Tom didn't have cancer or any other kind of disease; nothing that provided any warning that he was going to go. Not long after selling his three grocery stores for a good chunk of money, certainly enough that he could have done most anything with the rest of his life, Tom was back at work, this time as an employee at a Whole Foods store near where he lived. One day while carrying a crate of rutabagas to a customer's car, he keeled over from some sort of an aneurysm and within hours was gone.

Tom and I met in high school, two guys among ten who, from the beginning, just clicked. From our early days together playing cards in his parents' basement to the last game before he died in the house he built himself, our lives stayed banded together. We both married women we loved, adopted and raised children. Where I was often aloof and disinterested in strangers, not at all fond or skilled at connecting with people I didn't know, Tom made friends with everyone. He was genuine and warm and people universally liked him. Just the other day Laurie called and asked that I pick up a few things from the Rite-Aid near where we live. After hunting through the aisles awhile, I found most everything on Laurie's list and while I was checking out, the cashier, a young Hispanic woman whom I recognized as having worked there for a while, looked at me and, swear to God, said, "I sure miss your friend, Tom. Nice man. Nice, nice man. So sad." Me? I didn't even know her name. I nodded, grabbed my bag and left.

For a long time after Tom died, I was sad, sure. Just as much, though, I couldn't help but wonder why a guy with more than enough money to try something new, travel, anything—instead chose to go right back to getting up at four in the morning, five days a week, and doing exactly what he had done for most of his adult life. If that had been me, and I was able to put some real money in the bank, I was sure that I would not be grinding my days away in the divorce trenches.

It finally hit me one morning while I was sitting at my desk muddling through some poor fellow's bank statements and tax returns, pretty standard fare for a divorce attorney. Tom worked because that was what he had to do. More than that, though, it was what he wanted to do. He loved everything about his work, from the early morning wake-up calls to the chatter with all of the vendors and the endless stream of employee excuses and customer returns. Just because he could do something different didn't mean that he should do something different. And then there was me.

A day or two after that epiphany sunk in, I was killing some time, sipping my morning coffee and rummaging around a local gift shop. Tucked in the back of the store on a shelf with several of those signs that people like to read and laugh about but probably never actually buy was a small wooden plaque that said: *"LIVE LIKE SOMEONE LEFT THE GATE OPEN."*

I bought the sign and put it on my desk.

A few weeks after my buddy's death, I promised myself to try to look at things differently, try to change the way I felt about my work and find a new perspective—one that would enable me to see that in fact I was doing something meaningful. In the process, I told myself, I would find a way to enjoy what it was I did every day.

It's been close to a year now since I bought that sign. It's still in my office but has been moved from my desk to a credenza and now sits behind a pile of documents that make up next week's divorce trial. Actually, I can't say for sure that it is still there; I haven't looked at it for a while.

My friend is still dead. As for me, the gate is still closed.

SIX

Jess

My mom must have told the story about a thousand times about me trying to stab our dog, Sonny, with a fork when I was seven years old. She told my grandparents, my teachers, and all of my many therapists. Over the phone, at the playground, in the grocery store. Just about anyone and anywhere. I can't tell how many times I heard that story growing up. God knows how many more times she told it when I wasn't around. Personally, I never believed it since I love dogs, grew up with them, and would never be without one, even now, if I didn't have to live in a place that doesn't allow them.

That's not to say that I was an easy kid. Anything but.

Apparently, when I was in preschool, I refused to follow rules. I don't know exactly what rules I broke back then, maybe I didn't put the Legos back the right way or wouldn't stand in the right place in line. Who the hell knows?

Whatever it was, it was enough for my parents to okay my being evaluated by the preschool psychologist. From there, I was off and running through fifteen years or so of tests, shrinks, medications, and therapy that continued until I decided that I had enough and pulled the plug on most of it a few months before my dad died last year.

Even as a kid, I was acutely aware of the growing conflict between my parents over what to do, how to help, how to take care of me. How to "fix" me. While Kasey travelled the easy breezy, walk in the park kid route, mine was a bumpy, angry road. My mom always pushed for medication, while my dad pulled in the other direction, wanting to believe that I would be okay and better off without a bunch of prescription sedatives and mood stabilizers running through my veins. Ultimately, my mom won the battle and I spent the good part of my years from

18

childhood through my teens bouncing from diagnosis to diagnosis, treated with one drug and then the next. You name it; I had it. Attention deficit hyperactivity disorder. *Check*. Mood disorder. *Check*. Anxiety disorder. *Check*. Borderline personality disorder. Got that one, too. The list went on.

With every diagnosis came a pill. When one didn't work or caused some sort of unintended symptom, like I couldn't sleep or couldn't wake up, another plastic bottle was added to the collection in the cabinet above our kitchen sink. The list could have made some twisted alternate lyrics for a mad pharmacist singing Julie Andrews' "My Favorite Things" from *The Sound of Music*: "Ritalin to Seroquel to Adderall and Dexedrine. Abilify and Focalin and Lamictal and Prozac…"

I was always trying to find my way, walking through a house of mirrors. It was just that the mirrors weren't made of glass. They were made of drugs.

SEVEN

JB

At one time, I really did want to be a lawyer. I loved the old TV show, *Owen Marshall, Counselor at Law*. In those days, TV shows had theme songs actually written for the show (think *The Odd Couple* or *All in the Family*), not like the junk our kids watch now that hijack someone else's downloaded pop song to kick off a mundane twenty-three minute script. Owen's opening theme, even though I was only 11 or 12, always got me juiced. Horns trumpeted and drums pounded as Owen, in a crisp gray suit, white shirt and tie, strode across a grand lawn and then through a courthouse portico carrying nothing but a slim black leather attaché case under his arm.

No matter how bad things looked before the first commercial break, Owen's client was cleared and back on the streets before the closing credits scrolled across the screen. For some reason, as a teenager anyway, I thought that being a lawyer would be just like being Owen Marshall. I would wear a pinstripe suit, white shirt with cuff links, and dark tie. When I spoke, people would listen. People in the streets, people in my office, juries, and judges. Like Owen, I would not need to carry around too much; the way I carried myself would be enough. I would have an impact on people.

When I got to the University of Maryland, there was a professor who taught a pre-law class that students literally pushed and shoved to get in to. I say "pushed" and "shoved" because when I was in college, there was no online registration because, of course, there was no "online." We typed papers on typewriters, using Wite-Out for corrections, and waited in real lines to make copies at one of the two campus libraries for two cents a page. Similarly, we registered for classes the old-fashioned way; by heading to the old armory building armed with a fistful of number two pencils and a little pocket calendar to keep from signing up for two classes given at the same time. The armory was a cavernous yellow-brick building about two football fields long. With windows painted shut and no air-conditioning, the girls wore bikini tops for fall registration in August and big billowy L.L. Bean down parkas and vests for spring registration in January. I preferred August.

Registration took place over a two-day period, with seniors having first priority, followed by juniors, all of whom got to register and snap up the best classes on the first day. Freshmen and sophomores were relegated to day two, sparring mostly over the best times to take core classes and a few remaining electives that may have had only four or five slots left after the juniors and seniors picked through the best selections the day before.

Everyone, regardless of major or course of study, wanted to get into Dr. Carr's trial law class. Dr. Carr was a legend at Maryland; a famous local lawyer who was always on the news and in the papers, but who gave it all up to go back to his alma mater and become a college professor. Everyone raved about his classes; how he ranted and roamed across the classroom, plucking out students randomly and asking them to stand and answer questions in front of the entire class. His students were told not to bring books or notebooks to class; no pens or pencils either. "If you can't learn it by listening and participating, you aren't going to learn it," he told everyone.

With upper classmen getting priority, it wasn't until my senior year that I finally was able to get a spot in Dr. Carr's class, and even though it was at the crack at 8:00 am on Tuesdays and Thursdays, it didn't matter. The class was filled and I, like many others, made it my business to get there early to get a seat up front near the lectern.

Dr. Carr was a tall—well over six feet—portly balding fellow with brown horn-rimmed glasses and eyebrows that hung over them like window shades. Always in a sport jacket, slacks, and bow tie knotted just so, he was impressive without being intimidating.

At our first class, Dr. Carr made it clear that his class would be "student taught" and that he was not there "to lecture *ad infinitum* about the law" or "feed you young people with insipid reading materials to memorize and spit back out like some ticket taker at a circus."

I wasn't exactly sure what insipid meant and I certainly had never heard the phrase *ad infinitum* before, but boy was I hooked.

Almost every class started with a question about the reading we had been assigned. "Mr. Becker," he asked, one chilly Thursday morning, bounding from behind the lectern and toward my seat, two rows back. "I am the State's witness, having just testified that I heard screaming from your client's apartment just hours before the police found his wife beaten and mutilated."

He seemed to enjoy the scenario, having unusually lengthened the word to "*muuuuuutilaated.*"

I was hoping there was another Becker in the class.

"Now, of course, Mr. Becker, your client looks guilty as hell. His eyes are crazed, like a serpent, his hair scraggly, and despite your best efforts, he appears to the good men and women of the jury that he could kill each and every one of them with one swipe of his mammoth right paw.

"One more thing, there, Counselor," Dr. Carr said, subtly taunting me as the right edge of his lip twined up into his nostril.

"Although he appears guilty, and there was blood found and several others have already testified about hearing the sounds of arguing and fighting inside your client's apartment, well, the police, sadly for the prosecutor, they never recovered a body. His wife's body has never been found, yet your client is on trial for her murder."

Dr. Carr peeled off his jacket, pulled a chair in front of me, and plunked himself down, waiting, his eyes extending from their sockets, focused and spotlighted directly on me. "Go ahead, boy,

be the lawyer you say you want to be. I am the State's key
witness; having just testified about the grisly scene, blood everywhere and all the rest of that unruly business. Cross-examine
me."

For the next moment or so, I felt like I do right before I pass
out when giving blood or getting a shot. Everything was white
and my head was screaming; I blinked and tried my best to think.
What would Owen Marshall do? I asked myself.

What I thought was just a few seconds must have actually
been longer as the next thing I heard was Dr. Carr's voice, now
closer to me than he was when I last was seeing clearly. "Cross-
examination by silence, I see," Dr. Carr said. "Not at all effective,
young man."

A muted "sorry" was all I could muster in return. The rest of
the class, no doubt inordinately thankful that I had been thrust
behind the trial table for this little science experiment, remained
politely quiet.

My profound defeat palpable, Dr. Carr reached over and
slapped me on the shoulder. "Not to worry, my good friend.
You'll do better next time." He backed away, and returned to the
center of the room. "Let me tell you folks a story," he said.

*A man was on trial for killing his wife. During the prosecution's
case, witness after witness was called, each and every one testifying to
basic facts, all pointing to the clear and convincing guilt of the accused.
There had been arguing in the apartment. There was screaming in the
apartment. A gentleman from across the hallway heard the deceased
holler something about "a knife." When the police showed up a few days
later, blood was found on a large butcher knife, in the fibers of the
carpet, and on the defendant's shoes. The blood belonged to the
purported victim. A final witness was called, a longtime friend of the
couple. Distressed and weeping, this woman testified that on one
afternoon after leaving the apartment she stopped outside the front door
and listened to an argument inside. During that argument, the
defendant told his wife, "You bitch, I'm going to kill you."*

The defense attorney cross-examined none of the prosecution's witnesses, nor called any of his own, and instead waited for his closing argument to try to turn the jury against the overwhelming tide of a certain guilty verdict.

"Ladies and gentleman," he said. "You have seen all of the State's witnesses, each of whom points a finger at my client. You have heard from experts who have testified ad infinitum about bloodstains and butcher knives. The prosecutor has done a fine job. He has given you all that he has; and all of the evidence points to my client as the killer. One thing, though. One small thing. He hasn't shown you a body. Where is the victim? Where is Mrs. Blondell? For all you know, she could walk into this courtroom right this very moment."

Just as he said "moment," the defense attorney turned to the door in the back of the courtroom. It opened. The heads of all the jurors immediately swiveled toward the door to see if, in fact, the alleged deceased Mrs. Blondell was coming in. She wasn't. It was a fellow in a suit, employed no doubt by the defense attorney to assist in the charade. But his point, his point was made. Or at least he thought so. "See, look there," he shouted, tipping forward toward the jury. "Ladies and gentleman, you all looked when the door opened. Reasonable doubt! If you were without it, you would not have looked. You must therefore have reasonable doubt as to my client's guilt and with reasonable doubt, you must act as the law requires. You must find him not guilty."

The defense lawyer sat down, brimming with confidence in his client's acquittal.

After being instructed and sent to the deliberation room, however, the jury returned just moments later with a verdict. "Guilty," the foreman announced.

After the verdict was rendered, the defense lawyer was more than a bit perplexed and decided to pull aside the jury foreman. "How could you find him guilty? When the door opened, everyone looked. Everyone looked," said the lawyer.

The foreman smiled slightly and said, "Yes, we all looked, but your client didn't."

* * *

We left the class amid laughter and chatter, all of us totally charged up by our ninety-minute class with Dr. Carr and anxious to retell the story about that rat, Mr. Blondell, and how he murdered his wife.

I now had a new lawyer that I wanted to be, bow tie and all.

EIGHT

Jess

Everything about my mom seemed to be just so.

Exact.

She had thick dark brown hair that made her look as if she just stepped from a Vidal Sassoon commercial, even when she was getting us breakfast in the morning. When she got dressed, everything coordinated. Her necklace went with her earrings that tied into her belt that matched her shoes. Even until sometime in middle school, my mom dressed Kasey and me the same. I don't remember exactly when it started to bother me, just that at some point I had enough of the whole twin thing. There was one morning when she came into our bathroom while we were both getting ready for school. Mom was always happy to see Kasey, and since I was at my sink next to hers, some of the glow was inadvertently spread my way.

"What matchies are you going to wear today, girls?" she asked.

That's what she called our clothes. Matchies. Every time I think about that word, I get the taste of throw up in my mouth.

Anyway, my sister was thrilled. "Let me look. I will decide. Okay, mom?"

"You bet, cute girl!" Ugh. The two of them just scraped my middle school nerves. Kasey happily hopped out of the bathroom and past her bed into her closet.

I told my mother that I didn't feel well and thought I should stay home. She looked at me. Didn't take my temperature or even hold her cheek against my forehead like she always did with Kasey when she was sick. She just looked at me. The smile receded. Not to a frown. More like the look of indifference. Maybe it was relief.

"Okay, go back to bed" was all that my mom said before she

26

closed the door between us.

* * *

All through high school, my mom would wake up and make breakfast for us. My dad, who owned a few small grocery stores at the time, was generally gone hours before we got up and we would not see him until after school. There were so many mornings sitting at the counter having breakfast when I would look at my mom and then at Kasey next to me, both polished and perfect like the gleaming black granite countertops in our kitchen. Kasey was usually in some flouncy dress, her hair up in a big clip that was a staple of the standard outfit for the mainstream popular cheerleader types. She still used her knife and fork to eat her waffles, but only after spreading the butter just right, making sure that there was a little dribble in every little square. Dressed in some torn jeans that actually didn't come from the store that way, my favorite black high-top Converse sneakers and a sweatshirt from Hot Topic, I choked down whatever medications I was on at the time with some orange juice and a mouthful of Eggo waffle that I used my hands to eat. I didn't really like eating a syrupy waffle with my hands, but it drove my mother nuts and that was reason enough for me to do it. After breakfast, we would walk to the end of our driveway where the bus would pick us up. I would always get on the bus first, immediately heading as far back as I could go to find an empty seat by the window. Kasey plopped in front with her dress-alike friends and they chatted away for the entire ride to school. I sat by myself and looked out the window, as the trees and mailboxes scrolled past, quiet and jealous.

NINE

JB

It's an unfortunate irony. As my income has risen over the years, my desire to be at the office has correspondingly decreased. It's as if each phone call and client meeting, each deposition and court appearance, all drain just a little more gas from the tank, causing me to look for places to pull over, pause and stop; look for reasons to do just about anything other than practicing law.

In the past few years, I have been awfully creative in finding ways to avoid the office. I have coached Little League baseball; sometimes two teams at once, even though I don't have a kid who plays. I have served as an announcer at high school events, pretending as if I were working the PA at a pro football game. More than a few Friday afternoons have been spent in a nearby restaurant serving as a happy hour "guest bartender" pulling beers and watching baseball with whoever strolled in.

Even with my job fulfillment VACANCY sign flashing ever brighter as the years went by, until recently I was always particularly happy at home; my favorite profession is husband and father. And if I needed any reminders, with what I do for a living, I have seen more than my fair share of forty- or fifty-something men, otherwise successful and comfortable, blow up their lives because of some simmering sense of not being needed, not being what or where they wanted to be, or accomplishing what they should have; of some vague sense of having missed out, of life not being "good enough." With four daughters that looked to me to help with homework, go shopping, take them for ice cream — all of those normal things that most dads enjoy — it was always with my family that I felt like I made a difference, a positive difference, to someone. So what if the ten or twelve hours a day at the office were shit? I still knew that when it was over, I could go home and get hugged, do some coloring or homework, maybe get spilled on now and again.

Unfortunately, children grow into adults and now, my time as the center of my kids' lives has passed, *"left to vanish into the night,"* to borrow a lyric from Bruce Springsteen. There is no more "why do you have to go to work, Daddy?" morning sadness; similarly, the elated squeals of "Daddy's home!" and crashing into my knees in the kitchen at the end of the day have long since faded. When I come home now, I walk through that same laundry room door and every day see the inside of the doorframe, where we periodically marked each kid's height and the date. *"Whitney, June 2001"* in a dimmed red sharpie sits just above *"Sarah, 2003"* scratched in pencil.

It's been a long time since I marked the door, holding a ruler over the top of one of the girls' heads, telling her not to stand on her tippy toes so we could be sure that the line was drawn on just the right spot.

My wife, Laurie, who for years stayed home and was vested with the day-to-day responsibility of raising our girls while I built my law practice, has been able to pivot and go with the flow of life's changes. More than that, she has embraced those changes and gone back to her work as a therapist, working several nights a week with teenage kids. I feel envy, jealousy maybe, over her ability to move on with her life and take on different challenges in her now flourishing career.

Most mornings, I wake up the same way. I throw on shorts and a T-shirt, grab my dog, and head out for a walk through the woods. I tell myself that this day will be different. Today, I say, it will all change.

I will be relevant.

I will be useful.

I will matter.

TEN

Jess

Although my sister and I were adopted, people thought I looked like my father. Friends and sometimes people we would just meet at the park or a store or wherever would look and smile at the two of us, both with our hair swooped over from one side of our face to the other.

"Tom, that kid looks just like you," they would say. I liked it.

No one ever told me I looked like my mom. I liked that, too.

I think my fifth-grade graduation was the first time I realized that my relationship with my dad would always be different than with my mom. I never really understood the big deal about finishing elementary school, but since we now live in a society where everyone gets a trophy, the graduation from fifth grade into middle school was another reason for parents to get together, dress their kids in fancy clothes, and celebrate their impressive array of made-up accomplishments.

It was a tradition at Hoover Elementary that one soon-to-be graduate was chosen to give a speech at the ceremony each year. The teachers and our principal made a big deal over the Keynote Speaker Contest. There were posters in the fifth-grade hallway and starting in the middle of February, the morning announcements included a reminder that the competition was upcoming. Anyone interested would have to prepare a two-minute speech and give it to the panel of judges in our cafeteria sometime in early May, about a month before the big day.

I certainly had no interest in spouting on for two minutes about our parents, our teachers, or how much I would miss being a Hoover Hawk next year. There were not even teams in elementary school, so why was it we had a mascot? I asked everyone, teachers, other kids, even the janitor, Mr. Foncee, about that one. Most times I heard, "It's for school spirit, Jess," whatever that meant.

Actually, the most spirit I'd ever showed while at Hoover was when I ran around the playground calling Mrs. Kubow, the recess supervisor, a cunt. Since most kids my age never heard the word or knew what it meant, I figured I was safe. Mrs. Kubow knew the word and as one might guess, she did not take very kindly to a mouthy fifth grader running around cackling and screaming the word "cunt" all over the playground.

"Jess. You need to play nice," she said to me one day, for probably the millionth time.

"Okay, cunt!" I yelled back, as I skipped away across the blacktop.

After that, I was not allowed to go out to recess for a month and, even worse, had to sit through what would be the first of many a school conference with both of my parents, the principal, Mr. Keller, and Mrs. Kubow—the cunt.

Like him, Mr. Keller's office was unusually casual, especially for a school principal. He did not have a desk, but instead sat at a large high-backed wicker-style chair that looked like it belonged in Jamaica. Next to the chair was a knee-high round wooden table, littered with spiral notebooks and colored markers and pens. A cordless telephone rested on the left arm of the chair. A whiteboard was on the floor, leaning on the other side of the chair. My parents and I took our seats in the smaller chairs that curled in front of Mr. Keller.

"Mr. and Mrs. Porter, we love Jess here at Hoover Elementary. She is very bright and has enormous energy. Enormous energy," Mr. Keller repeated. "We are concerned, though, with her behavior. Her ability to sit in class, to stay focused," he said. "She could have real trouble next year. Things get tougher in middle school. In so many ways."

He spoke in an easy, friendly way, like a glass of milk. Tastes fine, but nothing too exciting or memorable about it.

"I know that Jess has had some therapy. She has an IEP and

has been on some medications, but I'm wondering if maybe you folks should talk to her doctor, see what else, uh, what other options there might be. She really is a handful," he went on.

An IEP is short for an "individualized education program." They are there not only to help kids with real, easy-to-see problems, like autism or cerebral palsy, but also for kids like me, called "assholes" by other kids and even some teachers. Us kids with learning disabilities, behavioral problems, maybe some mental illness or, in my case, a cursed combination of all three. In order to qualify for an IEP, the school pulls you out of class, makes you talk to a lot of people, and take a shitload of tests. And then, if you "pass," the school gives you some kind of code, and maybe even your school record is in a different-colored folder. I wondered what color my folder was.

Once I passed all the tests—yay!—the school gave me an IEP plan, supposedly designed to make me do better, get better grades. My plan was pretty simple. I sat in the front of class, got extra time on tests, and, my favorite of all, I was allowed to go to the bathroom whenever I wanted. I went a lot.

"I think, maybe, you should think about having Jess see this woman I know. She is great with kids. Especially girls," Mr. Keller said, handing my dad a purple business card.

"But she made honor roll," my dad said, taking the card from Mr. Keller.

"You mean I made honor roll," my mom said. "I have to force her to do her homework every night. She fights with me all the time. Most times, I end up doing the homework myself."

Mr. Keller nodded his head. I wasn't sure if he was okay with my mom doing my homework or pissed about it.

"Not all the time!" I jumped in.

Mom looked at me, the way she always did.

"Well, most of the time. Okay," I added, kind of whispering.

* * *

Not surprisingly, Kasey entered the fray and worked her little prissy ass off to try to win the Keynote Speaker Contest. She and my mom sat at the kitchen table night after night working on her speech. Once they had it written, Kasey would read it aloud in our bathroom, trying to make eye contact with herself in the mirror, and not look down at the words on the page. She asked me to listen, but I had no interest and instead whenever I saw her coming in with the two sheets of notebook paper, I would scurry out of the bathroom and into my room, closing the door.

It was a tough day at the Porter house when we got off the bus and Kasey had to tell mom that she didn't get picked to give the speech, losing out to a girl named Janet Hol-something. I couldn't pronounce her last name and the only thing I really knew about her was that she licked her chin obsessively and, as a result, walked around school with this big purple chapped arch under her lower lip. The thought that my Miss Perfect sister lost out to a kid who smeared ChapStick all over her face made me giddy.

"How could Janet Hupsackle beat you? Her face is about cracked off." I was one happy camper.

"Hulsapple is her name, Jess," my mom said, with my sister's head in her lap. "And that's not nice. At least your sister tried," she said, rubbing her hands through Kasey's hair, and in her own not-so-subtle way, reminding me that I had not.

* * *

As it turned out, my sister pulled herself together and gradu- ation—for her, anyway—went just fine. The class sang songs, there were a couple of talks by teachers about how they would miss all of us, how wonderful it had been teaching us kids, and so forth. Luckily, I was sitting in the second row, because I couldn't keep still. I was pulling on my hair, tapping my feet, and more than a couple of times, I reached over and tapped the shoulder of some kid named Charles, sitting next to me in a little blazer with khakis and a striped tie, like some sort of fifth-grade banker.

After Janet Hopsackle, Holsmopple, whatever—Christ, I still can't say it—after she gave her little talk about how we were all perfect flowers ready to bloom or some shit, Mr. Keller stood back up and started giving out awards.

First, he asked for each of the straight A students to stand and remain standing—of course, he told all the parents to hold their applause until all the awards were announced. A few kids stood up. After that, he announced the best science students, social studies students, and the same for other subjects. He announced the names of the best athletes, the best class helpers, pretty much anything you can think of—maybe even the best pretzel eaters— to ensure that every fifth-grade kid was standing at the end. That was the thing, though. After five, maybe ten minutes of announcing categories of "the best of" winners, I was still sitting down. I looked around, suddenly blinking away tears, wondering why I wasn't standing up. Just as I started to feel real sad, that tool Charles looked down and made a sniggering kind of laugh at me.

"Fuck you, banker boy," I said, as a kicked him in the left shin. He fell face first into the kid in front of him.

* * *

After the ceremony was over, I had some pictures taken with Kasey. My grandparents were there, so that was nice.

"How could you kick that boy?" My mom asked really loud, I think to make sure other people could see she was scolding me.

I don't think she expected me to answer.

I didn't disappoint her.

"Why do you have to do these things?" Now she was pinching my cheeks and twisting my face toward hers. I pulled away, holding the tears back. I didn't really know the answer to that one either.

My dad, who was always around at these kinds of things with his camera, was missing. After I gagged back a cry, I looked for him and asked my mom where he was.

"I don't know, Jess. He said he would be right back. I'm sure he will be. Now just stand there and try not to cause any more goddamn trouble," she said, making sure I could see her arm around Kasey's shoulders.

Dad showed back up just as we were being herded over to the cafeteria for a big celebratory lunch. He was carrying his camera in one hand, but in the other he had a blue ribbon, the kind they give to girls when they win the Miss America contest. I could tell that he must have taken it from Mrs. Grimes' art classroom, but wasn't sure why.

When he got to me, Dad put the ribbon over my shoulder and across my chest as if it was me who had just one the pageant. He had stuck some masking tape across the ribbon and written in a big red sharpie: "*Hoover's Future Superstar.*" I leaned my head into his waist and hugged him.

"Love you, Daddy," I said.

"Love you, too, Jessie girl," my dad said, pulling me into him.

ELEVEN

Jess and Jamie

"Hi, Jess. So nice to meet you," the lady said. She right away reached her hand out to shake mine. That seemed kind of weird, since I was still in middle school, but what the fuck, I grabbed her hand and shook back.

"My name is Jamie. Come on in," she said, opening the front door of her house.

My parents let me walk in first and they followed behind.

This place looked different from other doctors' and therapists' offices I had been in since I was in elementary school. One guy, Dr. Greishtag, I remember, kept calling me "Jesh" as if every word that ended in "s" had to sound like it ended in "sh." Other than a lot of "how are you feeling" kinds of questions, he didn't say much. I usually just looked at him and down at my shoes. He wrote a lot on a pad of paper, looked at his watch and me a bunch, then after a while called in my parents and wrote me a prescription. "Letsh try this one," he would say.

Another therapist I had, "Miss Amy" she liked to be called, talked to me like I was in a cartoon. In fact, when I went to see her, she had a fat little stuffed penguin that she called "Rollo." Miss Amy would not ask me questions, not like Dr. Greishtag. Instead, Miss Amy would say, "Rollo wants to know how you are doing today" or "Rollo wants to know how you feel about that."

Once I tried to answer Rollo's questions, but Miss Amy said, "Oh, no. Don't tell me, tell Rollo."

"Um, but Rollo is a penguin. A stuffed penguin," I said, at what turned out to be my last session with Miss Amy.

"But he wants to know!" Miss Amy said, with a daffy smile on her face. "Tell him! Tell Rollo!"

I had had enough.

"Screw Rollo," I said, just before I grabbed the furry little fucker by the neck and tore his head half off.

* * *

I liked that this lady's office was in her house. Jamie had a pretty foyer, with a curvy staircase right in the middle that had a brown-and-black leopard print carpet that covered the center of each stair, leaving some oak hardwood floor showing on either side. Off to the right was what I figured was a living room, with two identical couches facing each other and a table in the middle. There were family pictures all around; I assumed the people in the pictures were Jamie's family. Her husband. Her kids. I didn't remember any pictures of all of us at my house other than maybe when Kasey and me were babies.

"So, Jess, here's how I like to start."

Jamie was looking right at me, which at first made me feel awkward, but as she spoke more, I liked it. She was talking to me, not to my parents about me. Something about that made me feel good. When my parents first told me about seeing the purple card lady, I didn't want to come to therapy, but now that I was here, and Jamie seemed nice, maybe it wouldn't be so bad after all, I thought.

"This is about you, Jess," *Jamie said.* "You and I will be spending most the time just the two of us. But since it's your first time here, I call it an intake, I am going to meet with your mom and dad in my office for a few minutes and you can sit out here and play with my dogs." *She whistled and two fellows, one a fluffy light-colored golden retriever, with a pet store Nylabone in his mouth, the other a little white curly haired dog, ears flapping and tail wagging.*

"Jack is the golden. Lacy, who is in need of some grooming, is a bichon mix. My girls wanted a small dog, but she has really taken to my husband. Follows him everywhere," *Jamie said.* "Anyway, pet them and they will be your friends for life."

I reached my hands down and both dogs mushed themselves up against the couch, Jack licking my hand, Lacy working to shed some sweat off my ankle.

"Okay," *I said, as my mom and dad followed Jamie into the next room, connected but cut off by two glass-paned French-style doors.*

After my parents walked in, Jamie closed one of the doors, walked around to the other side and, bending at her knees, reached down to the floor, clicking on a little round cream-colored box, then smiled and closed the second door. The box sounded like the ocean and made a loud "shush" sound. It didn't take me long to figure out that the "shusher" was meant to ensure that whomever was sitting outside Jamie's office could not hear what was going on inside. It didn't bother me, and I knew what they were talking about anyway. Me.

After maybe fifteen minutes of being licked to death by Jamie's two dogs, my parents came out and my dad said, "Your turn, princess." My mom gave me her usual quick smile, like the kind you make to a stranger in an elevator, and sat down on the couch. My dad rubbed my head, and as I stood up, he sat down, taking my place with the two dogs.

Jamie's office was pretty neat. Except for the wall with the two doors, there were windows all around. I could tell that this room was not originally meant to be an office, and that probably made it a little less uncomfortable for me. In one corner, there was a baby grand piano, obviously not used too much since it was covered with folders and paper for her printer, which rested on the piano bench. Jamie had an old style looking desk facing the back wall of windows, with file cabinets on either side. Facing the desk, with their backs to the doors were two high-back turquoise leather chairs with a little table in between them. There was a wicker basket on the table, which I immediately noticed because it had a bunch of bright colored, rubbery kind of things in there.

Jamie must have seen me eyeing the basket.

"Go ahead, sit down and take one. I just got these delivered today," she said. "I call them fidget toys. Most people who come in here to talk to me wish they were somewhere else, so this gives them something to fidget with while we are together."

I sat down, grabbed a purple one with bug eyes on one end, and started fidgeting.

"So, what school do you go to?" Jamie asked.

Seemed like a dumb one to me. She's talked to my parents. More than once. She knows what school I go to. I wanted to like her so I let it go.

"*Martin Luther King,*" I answered.

"*How do you like it? What do you like to do outside of school?*" Jamie asked.

"*Which one do you want me to answer first?*" I responded. Smart-ass and all that.

"*Good point. It doesn't matter. I'm hoping we will see each other some more, so I'm just trying to get to know you. Not what your mom and dad may say about you,*" she said.

I liked that.

"*Well, school is fine, I guess. I have a lot of friends there. I don't really play any sports. I like to read, listen to music. That kind of stuff.*"

"*Nice. So do you have a best friend?*"

"*I have lots of best friends. Tess, Elizabeth, Allison. They're all my best friends.*"

"*That's really great,*" Jamie said. "*Most people are lucky just to have one best friend. And you have three!*"

The way her voice jumped up to a higher pitch on "three" was kind of irritating and at first I thought she was being fake, like she knew I didn't really have three best friends. I looked at her and she was smiling, in a real way, a nice way. That made me think she was sincere.

"*What do you guys do together? They come over, listen to music with you?*"

I thought for a second. "*No. Not really. They don't like to come over.*"

"*So do you go over their houses?*" Jamie asked me.

I squeezed the eyeballs of my fidget toy. "*No, we're pretty much just school friends,*" I said.

"*Oh. Are you okay with that?*"

She asks a lot of questions, this lady. But at least she was looking at me, and looking to be interested in what I had to say instead of taking notes. It also helped that I wasn't talking to an inanimate fur ball.

"*Yeah, I guess.*" I didn't really know what else to say. No one ever called me for a sleepover.

"*How do you and Kasey get along? Do you like being a twin?*"

"Like shit and don't give a fuck," is what I felt like saying. Instead, I took the easy way out and lied.

"Oh, she's fine. I don't think too much about being a twin, really."

Jamie nodded her head, as if to say, "I know that's a rash of shit, but will let it go for now."

"So, your parents tell me you are adopted," she asked.

I wasn't sure if that was a question or not, so I didn't say anything. I kept pinching the toy's eyes. The black centers of the rubbery eyeballs seemed to be getting bigger, the more I squeezed.

"What's that like for you?" Jamie asked. "Being adopted?"

That one was a question. I squeezed the eyes as hard as I could.

"Jess? I'm just wondering. How do you feel about being adopted?" she asked again, in a different way, as if I didn't understand the first time.

I twisted the eyeball harder and looked at her. "Feels like nothing, that's what," I said, just as the eyeball exploded shooting some gooey junk all over my hand.

"Sorry," I said, looking at Jamie. I was sorry. I didn't mean to break the thing. It just felt good squeezing.

Jamie laughed and leaned over, putting her hand on my shoulder.

"Seriously? No big deal. Look at this." She reached under her desk and slid out a good-sized cardboard box, pulling out a handful of more toys, even one or two with the wacky eyeballs.

"You are not the only one to break these things, believe me. That's why I keep about a hundred of them in here," Jamie said, taking a drink from her Diet Coke can.

"Okay," I answered, kind of happy that she wasn't yelling at me.

"And another thing, Jess. You aren't the only kid that's mad about being adopted either," she said, looking at me, straight on again, like she did when I was at the front door.

"Okay," I said again.

TWELVE

JB

Today, I really wanted to get the hell out of the office. My day started well enough; up around 6:00 am and a long walk through the woods with my dog. After a little breakfast and run through the sports page, I went upstairs and found my wife naked in front of the mirror, leg up on the counter, spreading some moisturizer up her thigh and getting ready to head to the gym. Not wanting to disappoint or appear out of character, I made my usual attempt at a quickie; I stood behind her, pressed against her ass and grabbed her breasts.

Not the least bit impressed and even less interested, Laurie removed my hands from her breasts, turned, gave me a quick kiss and said, "You're so funny. Love you, but not happening."

Disappointed as usual, but hardly surprised, I took a shower and headed out to the office. Like every other day, I was at my desk by 8:30 am with my day's to-do list staring at me from my new iPad mini, wishing I were somewhere else.

The list was nothing out of the ordinary for a day that I didn't have to be in court. After returning a half hour or so worth of emails, I was going to be stacked up with a full morning of back-to-back appointments. First, a phone conference with Teri Dennis at 9:00 am to review her Answers to Interrogatories, then a call with Jackie Spencer at 10:00 am to catch me up on her plans for a SWAT move to Connecticut when her husband leaves for his boys weekend in Vegas at the end of the month. Forty-eight hours, fill a moving truck, and she'll be gone from the state. If she tells him in advance, according to the law, all she can hope to leave with is her purse and the cash in her wallet. At 11:00 am, Beth Tanner comes in to discuss ditching her collaborative divorce and hiring me to start litigation against her husband who it appears has been anything but "collaborative" over the last several months, starting with hiding a good chunk of marital money.

Basically, a collaborative divorce is a natural outgrowth of the inherent desire that most people have to "just get along." Instead of the divorcing spouses lawyering up, firing off nasty letters, or filing a lawsuit, the parties each hire their own collaborative divorce lawyer, who, yes, is to be representing them, but is also fully committed to the success of the collaborative process. Not only are there lawyers, but the parties also bring in and retain (i.e., pay for) a series of other professionals—child specialists, financial neutrals, even folks labeled "divorce coaches." If only those folks had taken the time to find marriage coaches instead, more families might stay together. Of course, if that happened, I might be in a different line of work.

Everyone involved must express absolute dedication to the collaborative process—working together to decide on the best plan for the family unit—even the lawyers who, in the event that the process fails, can no longer represent their clients. As a result, the clients are forced to start anew and, of course, pay another lawyer to take their case. Despite sincere efforts to the contrary, the new lawyers may just go ahead and further fuck up the already fucked-up lives of their clients.

The idea of collaboration itself, while all good intentioned and occasionally successful, often leads to exactly what the couple intended to avoid in the first place—divisiveness, bickering, delay, and a pile of legal bills.

Although I understand the philosophy and appreciate the sentiment, I am not a huge fan of the collaborative divorce concept. I figure that I can settle any case where the parties really want it settled, without the rules and strings of the collaborative team and without all the nonsense of meetings, status memos, divorce coaches, and the like. And if I can't, the other side knows that I can go to court and my client doesn't have to get herself another lawyer.

Ironically, some of the most difficult bastards I have ever had to deal with are the spouses of folks whose divorce started "collaboratively" but eventually found their way to my office after months of frustration, inaction, and failure. For better or worse, all I have to sell is my time, and at almost five hundred bucks an hour, these collaborative failures can be treasure troves for me.

* * *

At about 9:00 am, one of my assistants, Pam, poked her head around my doorway and said hello. She was wearing a short gray-and-white floral dress from Free People, and some strappy high heels that, on anyone but her, would be tough to pull off in an office setting. She is always put together, I guess you would call it; her makeup is just right, not too much, just soft and pretty, with maybe a touch of lipstick. At maybe five feet tall on a hot day, Pam is always in big heels and I, for one, appreciate the view.

Pam and I have known each other since college. One of the many "It girls" who wouldn't look my way in those days, Pam married a good friend of mine, and with their kids grown and off to college, she came to work for me and the firm a few years back. Although she sits up front in the reception area and greets clients when they come in, Pam has become a rainmaker in her own right, referring new clients my way, keeping them happy and comfortable when they are here, and staying in touch with a quick call or email when I am not available or, as has become more often the case, just not interested.

I started calling her LG a while ago; it's short for "Little General." "Little" because she is and "General" because she is exceptional at telling everyone what do. I have told her husband, my good friend Vinnie, on more than one occasion that "the best thing about Pam working for me is that she goes home to you." He and I laugh about it, but I can also see in his eyes that he knows exactly what I am talking about.

"What's going on, Broshie?" Pam asks. "Broshie" is her version of "Bro," a nickname I have had since high school.

"Same old bullshit, LG," I answer, feeling short tempered and irritable for no other reason than I am in the office and behind my desk.

"Seriously?" she says, stepping closer to my desk.

Her legs look great today. I know she's married to my buddy and I have a gorgeous woman at home, but it's hard not to leer, just a slight bit, as she puts her hands on her hips and bends toward me, in a way that I know exactly what is coming.

"What are you complaining about? A day of work? You just got back from California, you're going away again next month, and poor you, got to work in the office today. So sad for you," she says.

I start to get angry; after all, this little general in heels works for me, not the other way around. The feeling doesn't last long, though.

"You're right," I say.

She smiles at me, the Little General, taking it all in. I have once again surrendered to her infinite common sense. She is right, and I need to stop whining.

Just as she is about to say something, thankfully the phone rings and she spins on those heels, heading toward the front to answer. Great ass, that one, I say to myself.

Before I turn back to my computer, Pam is back in my office.

"Yes?" I ask. "Here to kick some more sand my way?"

"No. Actually, it's Lianne. Lianne Porter is on the phone. She wants to talk to you." She's making a face that says "sorry" without actually saying anything.

Garnering some sympathy, I must have responded with a look that said, "Please no, anything but this."

"Just talk to her, Broshie. It will be fine," Pam said. "Oh and by the way, you're up to an M."

I looked at her, not knowing what she meant at first then

realizing that she was referring to one of the options in our ongoing "kill, fuck, or marry" game that we have played outside the office on a few of our double-date nights. Either listing strangers or even better, the name of a person we all know, one of us will ask the other, "Kill, fuck, or marry?"

I always assumed that if I were the subject of the question, Pam would choose K as my fate. So when she gave me an M, that was big news.

"Really?" I asked, suddenly proud of myself. "I thought for sure I was a K."

"Nope. You're definitely an M," she said.

Since the M by nature has to include the F, all of the sudden, moronic male that I am, my biceps felt bigger, and I sat up a bit taller. I was suddenly feeling chipper and ready to face the day.

"Put her on," I told Pam.

THIRTEEN

Jess

My mom, Lianne Porter, grew up as Lianne Cohen in a conveniently observant Jewish family in Silver Spring, a sprawling DC suburb in Montgomery County, Maryland. "Convenient" because like a lot of Jewish families, I think they observed the easy holidays—Hanukkah, for example, and went to synagogue twice a year, for Rosh Hashanah and Yom Kippur. She and my dad met in high school. My dad was raised a Catholic so they kept their dating secret from mom's parents until their senior year. I don't think that either of them really ever went out with anyone else. Both my parents went to the University of Maryland, my mom graduating in four years with a degree in textiles, for some inexplicable reason. I can't even imagine why anyone would go to college to study the dynamics of how wool is dyed or polyester stretched. I don't know if she worked or not after college, but I do know that it took my dad a lot longer to graduate. Both of his parents died when he was in high school. After they died, my dad and his brother Paul lived with some relatives until they graduated. Dad never talked much about my Uncle Paul, other than to tell me, when no one else could hear, that Paul was a douchebag.

Dad worked full time through college at a series of local grocery stores and finally graduated, as he called it, on the six-year plan. At some point during college or soon after, he converted to Judaism and he and my mom got married.

From what I remember them telling me, my mom and dad lived with my mother's parents for a couple of years after getting married. My grandparents, Harold and Shirley Cohen, came from different sides of the tracks, as Pops used to say. My grandfather liked us calling him "Pops," not because it was a somewhat traditional grandparent reference, but because he said it reminded him of the cereal that Grammy would not let him eat after he was diagnosed with diabetes. No matter how many times he told us, "It wouldn't be right for you girls to call me 'Sugar' so 'Pops' is good," I still thought it was funny.

Pops was proud to be a lawyer. I knew that because he told us, I think, almost every time we saw him. He and Grammy would come over to the house for dinner every Sunday night, something I really looked forward to each week. Mom was a pretty good cook but on Sundays in the summer, my dad usually took over, firing up about half a dude ranch full of meat on the grill. If I close my eyes real tight, I can still see him, just the way I used to, stooped over the charcoal grill, smoke billowing so thick that I could barely make out his red apron, with a long-since scorched Maryland Terrapin on the front. But for the way he would swipe his hair from one side of his face to the other, it was hard to tell he was my father.

There were no vegans in my family and, like Dad, we all loved our red meat. Otherwise, a birdlike eater, even Kasey would down one of the cheeseburgers that Dad made by hand, rolling the ground beef and then pinching the cheese inside the meat rather than on top, like cheeseburgers everywhere else. Mom and Grammy ate the steaks, done Pittsburgh-style: charred on the outside and rare in the middle. Like Pops, though, my favorites were the Roxy dogs. A Roxy dog was really nothing special or out of the ordinary, just a regular Hebrew National hotdog, but with both ends sliced and quartered, so when they cooked, the "tails" would curl and crisp, like overdone French fries.

When the tails were done just right, Dad would call Pops and me over to the grill.

"You two ready for a little nibble?" he'd asked us.

Pops would peer over the grill first. "Not 'til they're squealing, Tommy boy," he said.

By "screaming," Pops meant that the roxies were cooked so well that the juice was popping out of the skin and making a snaky hissing kind of noise. Once they "squealed," Pops taught us, they were ready.

"There you go. Break us a little nibble, Tommy boy," he said.

Once Pops gave the word, Dad would pull off three of the tails with his fingers, one for each of us. After years of this same ritual, I mimicked the two of them and would nod my head "mmmhmm," in unison with Dad and Pops.

"Your dad can sure cook," Pops said to me. "And that's good, but Jessie girl, he works too hard. Getting up at three am, carrying boxes of fish and other *chazerai* all day, that's for the loony birds," Pops said.

Whatever "chazerai" was, it didn't sound good. And my dad, he toted it around all the time at work, if you believed Pops.

"When you grow up, you need a profession. Be a lawyer, like your Pops. If your back hurts or your hip goes out or you have some other problem when you get old, and you will, you always have your brain. I know lawyers that are seventy years old and still working as hard as they did when they were thirty. These are smart people, Jessie girl. Trust me," he said.

The fact is that I did trust Pops. I also loved that he called my dad "Tommy boy" and me "Jessie girl." But the idea of me being a lawyer, sitting behind a desk, and wearing a long wool skirt and blouse with a ribbon closing up the neck? Talking on the phone all day?

Shit, I barely made it through high school.

FOURTEEN

JB

Hearing that Lianne was on the phone quickly snapped me back to reality and away from the brief feeling of pride by being included on Pam's M list. Lianne and I had never gotten along, from the time we met in high school, through college, and even after she and Tom got married. When I first met her, I immediately didn't like her but figured that Tom would move on sooner or later, to someone fun and warm and decent, like him. She was always trying to keep him away from his friends, usually under some promise, at least that's what Tom thought, that if he spent time with her instead of his friends, he would get laid. I think she kept that promise just enough to ensure that Tom would do whatever she asked.

After they adopted the girls and Tom started to make some real money, Lianne became one of those people who, no matter what someone else does or has, she has done more and has better. It didn't matter if you took a trip around the world that lasted six months; her night at a Holiday Inn Express outside of Baltimore was all she would talk about. Rarely one to ask about your life, your children, or your work, Lianne nattered on endlessly about her latest find at Nordstrom, her recent redecorating project, her boob job. I never understood Tom's willingness to pay for the new breasts—by that time, she hardly let him see them anyway, much less enjoy any other of their obvious benefits.

A few days after the funeral, Lianne and the girls came to my office to meet with my law partner and discuss Tom's will and how to handle some of the estate and probate issues. While most folks with Tom's money often leave everything to their surviving spouse, or, if they want to, carve out a separate pocket of money for their children, even if those children are adults, they often do it via some sort of a trust to ensure that their kid does not spend all the money at once. Tom, whom I knew had a special relationship with Jess, put a share of her money into a trust for her benefit until she was thirty, but the rest he gave directly to her. That really irritated Lianne, since all of Kasey's inheritance went into a trust, but more to the point, because she did not care much for Jess.

Tom's different treatment of the kids was a bit unusual, no question, especially since I knew he loved both girls. With Lianne long since having forged a close and "favorite child" relationship with Kasey, I knew that he saw himself as Jess's protector. My guess, and that is all it is since we never talked about it, and I didn't feel comfortable asking my law partner who drafted the will to betray a confidence, was that he must have known Lianne's conflict with Jess was likely to worsen after he died. I assumed that he did not want to leave Jess with nothing until she was thirty in the event that Lianne decided to toss her out of the house, something I knew she had done several times since Jess was about sixteen.

I slid on my Bluetooth headset, took a sip from my favorite mug, banana yellow from the Badass Coffee Shop, and hit the connect button.

"Hi, Lianne. How are you doing?" I asked, as evenly as I could.

"Fine. Thanks for asking." Monotone. Unemotional. "You know that the unveiling is coming up, right?" she asked me.

"Yes. I got the email blast. I'll be there. Everything okay?" I was certain that she wasn't calling me to be sure that I would attend. If given a choice, I knew, she would much prefer that none of Tom's friends showed up.

"Yeah, fine. Pretty much. I actually wanted to ask if you would call Jess. Make sure she is coming," Lianne said.

I knew that Jess had left Maryland shortly after her father died and moved to Florida with her friend. Beyond that, I had not kept in touch with her and I didn't really know what was going on.

"You haven't talked to her?" I asked.

"No," she answered. No explanation.

"Okay, so why don't you call her yourself?" I asked. "I'm not sure it's my place. Plus, how would she know if no one has told her?"

"She and I haven't spoken since she took off and she knows because she got the same email that everyone else did," Lianne said.

Nice way to treat your kid, I thought. Send an email about her dead father's unveiling.

What I felt like doing, frankly, was to tell Lianne, for once, to act like a mother and call her kid. Get the girl a plane ticket; get her up here. I didn't.

"Listen, JB, I'll pay for the ticket. I just have no intention of calling her, the way she treated us," Lianne said.

I almost asked what it was exactly that Jess had done to justify months' worth of the silent treatment, but thought the better of it.

"Tom would want her there, so she should be there, that's all," Lianne said.

The rest of it aside, whatever it was, she was right. "Sure, I'll get her there," I said.

"Here, write this down," Lianne said, giving me Jess's cell phone number.

Once I read the number back to her, Lianne said, "Yeah, that's it" and hung up.

FIFTEEN

Jess

It seemed I was always angry with my mom. Or she was always angry with me. Probably both. But my dad, that was different. I loved him. Seriously, I did. Every minute of every day. I know it sounds creepy and weird, but even into my teens and early twenties, right up to when he died laying in the hospital bed with me next to him, he was the center of my world. It's like when you get a new puppy. There is one person in the family who feeds, nurtures, and takes care of her. The one who walks the dog and lies down in the dog bed with her. I read that in the dog universe, that person is called the alpha. That's what my dad was to me. My alpha.

* * *

My dad had lots of things that he loved. For some reason I still haven't figured out and probably never will, he loved my mom. Of course, he loved my sister and me. He literally lusted over food and went nuts over some weird TV shows. One of his favorite shows was *Star Trek*. Not the "*Next Generation* bullshit," as he called the later version of the show; it was the original 1960s series with Captain Kirk, Spock, Dr. McCoy, and all the rest that he adored. Back in the days before Netflix, he would sometimes find a rerun on some cable network and as soon as he did would come looking for us to watch with him. Kasey was never too interested, preferring one of those sappy Disney Channel sitcoms. For me, it was great. I would drop whatever I was doing and squeeze next to him onto the couch in our family room, being sure not to miss the opening part of the show.

"You ready, Jessie girl?"

"Yep, let's do it!"

Just as Captain Kirk's voice would come on, we talked right along with him, in our deep and very ominous *Star Trek* voices: "These are the voyages of the *Starship Enterprise*. Its five-year mission to explore strange new worlds and new civilizations — TO BOLDLY GO WHERE NO MAN HAS GONE BEFORE!"

We always screamed the last part and then settled in for the episode. Sometimes while the show was on, I would look over at him while he was watching. He was always so involved in the show, even if it was like the twenty-fifth time he had seen that particular episode. My mom thought he was weird. Kasey did too. Not me. I thought he was great.

I think about him a lot. Every day. Sometimes, when I still can't sleep, I will queue up an old episode on my laptop and repeat the Captain Kirk introduction, whispering the "where no man has gone before" opening and pretending my dad is there with me.

SIXTEEN

Jess and JB

"Hello, this is Jess."

"Hey, Jess. It's me, JB. I mean, sorry, Uncle Bro."

"Hi, Uncle Bro! How you doing?"

"I'm good, Jess. I hear you're living down in Florida now."

"Yeah. Moved down last year after Dad died. My friend was down here, said she could help me with a job."

"So, where you working?"

"I'm a bartender at this little bar here in Jones Beach, The Shipwreck. Whole place looks like a boat inside, a little weird. Ropes hanging everywhere and a dance floor that looks like the deck of an old pirate boat or something. Anyway, and every hour between four and closing I have to ring a bell, like the one they used to have on, I don't know, the *Pinta* or the *Santa Maria* maybe, so everyone knows they have five minutes for four-dollar shots. It's more of a local's place than tourists, but I make pretty good money. They play a lot of Jimmy Buffett, but mostly seventies and eighties rock. I think I know every word to every Eagles song ever recorded. You'd like it. Dad, too."

"Sounds great, Jess. My kind of place."

"Oh, yeah, you know that nineties Cheryl Crow song? The one that starts with 'this ain't no disco, this ain't no country club either'? They play it every night around midnight and all the girls who go up on the deck of the boat to dance, get free Buds. Pretty fun."

"Girls dancing and drinking Budweiser. Sounds perfect to me."

"I know, right? I thought about all you guys as soon as I came in for the interview. It just seemed like a place where you and Dad and the other guys would be sitting at the bar, downing Rolling Rocks or whatever. Oh yeah, you used to be a bartender, right?"

"Yeah, back in college and law school. Fun job. Loved it. People gave me a hard time; I bounced them out. I hear the same problems now, but I get paid a lot more for it. So can't throw them out."

"Funny. Oh, well. Maybe you should come down here and take a few shifts. Might like it."

"I might take you up on that, Jess. In the meantime, though, I wanted to talk to you about something."

"Figured you weren't calling just to say hi. This is a new number I got when I moved to Florida so Mom must have given it to you. I called her after I got down here and left her a message so she would know how to get a hold of me. She didn't call back."

"Uh, yeah, she called me this morning. She asked me for a favor, so I'm, well, I guess I'm going to ask you."

"Okay, what?"

"Your dad's unveiling is just over a month away and your mom was worried that you wouldn't be there. She said she sent you an email, but did not hear back."

"Yeah, that's right. She sent me an email."

"Okay, so are you coming up? She told me to let you know she would pay for the plane ticket."

"Not interested. I said goodbye to him at the funeral. I don't need to come back and do it all over again. Plus, I don't feel like talking to her or seeing my sister. I have a new life, I've moved on."

"It's important to her that you be there, Jess."

"Well, maybe she should have sent me a card or, wait, how about actually maybe even called me on the phone?"

"I don't know, Jess. I really don't. But the bottom line is that she is your mom and it's about your dad, not her, and not you. You can be up and back in Jones Beach slinging drinks and ringing that bell in a couple of days." It got really quiet on the other end.

"I just, I don't know. Shit."

I waited, trying to think of what else I could say when Jess spoke up again.

"Hey, Uncle Bro, can I ask you something? I mean I've been thinking about something since I've been down here."

"What's that?"

"Like, I've been wondering, maybe I wasn't meant to be adopted. Dad and Mom should have taken Kasey and left me behind with my birth family. Maybe I wouldn't have been so fucked up."

"Come on, Jess. You can't mean that." Even as I said that, I could almost feel Laurie rolling her eyes as me, saying that I shouldn't be telling Jess what she means. Fumbling for the reset button, I started over. "You meant everything to your dad. It didn't matter that you were adopted. You could have been from Mars for all he cared. He loved the shit out of you."

"But he's dead."

She had me there. "He is, yes."

"Uncle Bro, I want to try to find my birth family. You think you can help me?"

I should have seen this coming. "Why don't you just ask your mom? She must have some information that could help you."

"I don't think she stayed in touch with my birth mother, so other than knowing I was born in Pittsburgh to some people that didn't want me, I don't have much to go on. Plus, I figure you could go to the courthouse and get me whatever records are there. That's a start, right?"

"Sure, it's a start. But you're talking about twenty-three years ago. A lot happens to people in twenty-three years, Jess."

"No shit, Uncle Bro. Will you help me?"

"I still think you should call your mom, talk to her about it."

"I'll send her an email." I could hear her sucking in her breath. "So, will you help?"

"It's not really my thing, Jess, but I'll tell you what. Come on

56

up for a few days before the unveiling, and let's talk about it."

"I don't want to spend my whole life wondering, thinking I should have been someone else. Tell me you'll help me and I'll come up."

"I'll help you."

"What's mom's credit card number?"

SEVENTEEN

JB

One thing she said stuck to me like gum you can't get off your shoe. *"Figured you weren't calling just to say hi."*

Why not? Why didn't I call, just to say hi? I knew about her troubles with her mom and sister. I knew that Tom was worried she would become isolated, separated even from the rest of her family. He was right. She had packed up and moved a thousand miles away from them. I could have helped, couldn't I? I could have done something. I could have had her stay with Laurie and me; at least tried to talk to Lianne. I don't know what I would have said, or done even. Just something.

And now, a situation presents itself; I can help. Instead of just telling her yes, though, the lawyer in me took over. I brokered a deal.

"I'll do this, Jess, if you do that."

"I'll help you find your birth family if you come up to Maryland."

What a dick, I thought.

Forgetting the Bluetooth, I picked up the phone and called her back.

"Hi, Uncle Bro. That was quick. You want to make sure I bring a dress? Be nice and polite to everyone?"

"Actually, no. I want to help you find your birth family, Jess, and I don't see why I need to wait a month to get started. I'm going to get the court records pulled, then I will come on down and we can look at them together. I wouldn't mind getting out of this office for a while anyway. Wear anything but these same oxfords for a day or two," I said.

"Oxfords?" she asked.

"They're men's shoes. Don't worry about it. Sorry." I was rambling.

"Uh, okay, sure, Uncle Bro," Jess said, seeming to poke a little fun at me. Like her Dad used to.

"I'll be down in a few days. Don't worry, I'll find you. The Shipwreck, right?" I asked.

"Yep. Every night but Sunday," she said.

"See you soon," I said, as I hung up.

* * *

"Better call Laurie, don't you think?" Pam asked, her head craned around my doorway.

EIGHTEEN

Jess

I was excited to tell Macy about my phone call with Uncle Bro. Never in my whole life, growing up, did I ever really have a best friend. There were girls in school that depending on the day, were nice to me but no one who I knew really liked me. You know, someone who called me because she wanted to talk to me, not because her mom set up a play date or she had nothing better to do and I had a great basement for kids to hang out in, with a big TV, old-fashioned pinball games, and even a dance floor with a disco ball.

I was so different from my sister, who had friends falling out of everywhere. It seemed strange to me how easy it was for her to make friends. I mean Kasey was always so quiet; it wasn't as if she was really friendly or funny or anything. She smiled a lot, I guess, but other than that, she never had much to say and was happy just hanging around, doing whatever anyone else wanted to do. Maybe that was it—her ability to "go with the flow," as my therapist called it, that made it easy for her to find friends, or I guess easy for them to find her.

There were so many times that I sat on my itchy gray carpet and cracked the door from my room upstairs, just to listen to them talk. I even whispered to myself, pretending that I was part of the conversation, often laughing with the girls, as if I too were right there, at the kitchen table, talking about cheerleading, a senior boy, or which party we should go to that Saturday night.

* * *

Macy came into my life as abruptly as my dad left it. I have never been one to think much about God, because if I did, I would probably come to the conclusion that God was a jerk, for giving me all these problems and issues; for making me spend day after day in my room, for taking my dad away from me, for being adopted, for being bad and difficult and obnoxious, for being me. For. For. For.

Now, thinking back on it, it does seem like meeting her, getting to be her friend was part of some sort of planned, preconceived connection.

But for my going back to see Jamie a few days after the funeral, I would have never met Macy, and, for all I know, never had a real, true friend. It's funny because before that afternoon I hadn't seen Jamie in I don't know how long, and although I spent a lot of time yelling and blaming and being pissed in her office over the years, I can never thank her enough for sending me on the trail that led to Macy.

NINETEEN

Jess and Jamie

"Jess, it's so good to see you," Jamie said, opening the door.

"Thanks," I said, avoiding eye contact, looking past her and into the house. "You, too."

"I'm sorry about your dad," she said.

"Yeah, me too," I said.

"Your mom called and told me. Come on in," she said, as I was already brushing by her, toward the shusher and into the office.

We stepped into her office, which was pretty much the same as when I was last here. I flopped onto one of the familiar turquoise leather chairs that were now a little more worn and faded. I tried to think when I last saw Jamie. Oh yeah, after I got the tattoo while out drinking and getting high and I passed out in the yard for like the two hundredth time and, no, I really don't want to think about it.

Most of the therapy I could live without, but I was comfortable here. I knew Jamie would come at me eventually, asking about my feelings, whether I was trying to get along with my mom and my sister, whether I was cutting again, that kind of thing. With my dad gone, I felt like talking to someone, and it wasn't like I had a lot of choices.

"You got a new computer," I said, noticing the MacBook Air on her desk. "Nice."

"You're cutting again," she said, noticing that I was wearing long sleeves, when it was close to ninety degrees outside.

"Just once since he died," I said, as if it was nothing. Fact is, I felt like going home and doing it again. Now.

"How long had it been?" she asked.

"A while, really. Months, maybe a year. I don't know, but I was feeling okay. I just didn't feel the need."

"Okay, so why, now?" Jamie asked.

"My father is dead. I assume that has something to do with it," I snipped, feeling kind of angry, but not knowing why.

Not even slightly reacting to my jumping at her. "It's perfectly normal to be angry after someone you love dies," she said.

"Well, I don't know why I would be angry. It's not like he did it on purpose," I said, trying, maybe, to be funny, but failing miserably.

"Have you ever heard of Elisabeth Kübler-Ross?" Jamie asked.

"I didn't go to college. What do you think?" I answered, now aiming my trigger finger temper right at Jamie.

"Listen, being mad is fine, being mad at me is fine. But you should at least know why. Kübler-Ross was a psychiatrist who researched the effects of death on the survivors and found that there are five stages, or emotions, that people can feel after the death of someone that they love. Not everyone feels all of the emotions, and there are certainly others. Also, some people feel other things as well, but her work is pretty much still held in high esteem by us 'shrinky' folks. It's called DABDA, which stands for the stages: denial, anger, bargaining, depression, and acceptance. You, my girl, are experiencing the anger piece."

"Okay, that's great to know," I said. "But really what difference does it make? I'm angry? So what? Why shouldn't I be?"

"Well, like anything else, knowing the 'why' can help with the 'what,' if you know what I mean," she said.

"Fuck, here we go again. Seriously, Jamie, I don't know what you are talking about. My dad died, I cut myself. It felt good; made me feel better, if you really want to know. So what is it that you are trying to tell me?" I asked, rubbing my right hand on my left sleeve.

"You are so full of shit, Jess. You know exactly what I am saying," she said, looking right at me, smiling in that "not fooling me" way she does, and resting her chin in her palm.

"Okay, fine." I surrendered. I had had enough of this irritating psychobabble anyway. "So, my dad died. I'm angry. Good for you. You figured that out. And what am I doing to cope with his dying and my being angry? I am cutting. I get it. You happy?"

"No. Not really," she said. "I'm glad that you put down the 'I didn't go to college and therefore I'm stupid' crutch, but you need to see that cutting is not going to help how you feel. It's a negative—"

"—coping mechanism." I finished the sentence for her. God knows, I had heard that term more than a few times in this room over the years.

Her voice got softer. "Listen, Jess, there is no right or wrong way to grieve. No one tells you how you should feel or how you should act when someone you love dies. And I know how close you felt to your dad. I do. You just can't deal with it by cutting yourself again," she said.

"So, okay, what exactly is a positive way to deal with it? I mean my life wasn't exactly all that great before, but now it really sucks," I said, feeling like I had no place to go. I was down and that was where I was going to stay.

"I want you to try this young adult group down at the community college. It's really great, run by a psychologist I know, his name is Dr. Palmer. It's mostly people your age. Some are adopted. Some lost parents, some have drug issues, and some are just trying to find themselves. A lot of young people have struggles, Jess, and it can help to talk about things. Drives home the fact that you are not alone. I have heard terrific things and I know he has a couple of openings. Not high pressure, just mostly people in their low twenties, talking and listening. Nothing specific. I think you would like it."

"Sounds great. Nothing specific. Nothing in common except everyone is fucked-up," I said.

"Well, that's one way to look at it," Jamie said. "Of course, you could also look at it as an opportunity to move forward and feel better. It might be good to meet some other people your age. Maybe talk some, get to know them. Who knows? Maybe you will make a friend or two."

"I just don't see how a therapy group is going to make me feel better," I said.

"Jess, you have to work on getting your awesome back," Jamie said, as if it made sense to anyone but her.

"Okay, sure, I'm right on that," I said. This time, I really had no idea what she was talking about.

She looked at me and pitched her eyebrows up into an arch.

"Let me tell you what I mean. You know when you see that five-year-old boy strutting around in his front yard with nothing on but cowboy *boots and a superman cape pushing a yellow plastic lawn mower? He is so proud; so happy. You just know it. He is feeling awesome. No one has told him he looks ridiculous, that he should wear something else, pants maybe. Not to mention that Superman was not a cowboy. And he probably never cut the grass. It just doesn't matter; the kid is feeling it, it's pulsing through his little body, he's got it—his awesome. That's what you need to get back. You are a great kid—funny, smart, and, if I were a twenty-something boy, not too tough on the eyes either. And God knows, energy that never runs out. You have awesome; you just need to find it," she said.*

"I don't have a Superman cape," I said, nodding. I did kind of get what she meant, though.

"I do have some great western boots though, Frye's like my dad," I added, trying not to perk up too much.

"Well, there you go," she said. "Put those boots on and go find it."

My time was up; I gave her a hug.

I didn't exactly know how I was going to do it, or even if I ever had it, but I was going to do what Jamie said. I was going to get my awesome back.

TWENTY

Jess

I got to Room B-223 a few minutes late. For once, I actually would have been on time but not having been in a school in a while, I got confused finding my way from one lettered hallway to the other. The door was open, and I turned sideways to pinch myself through, hoping not to be noticed, at least not right at first. The first thing I saw was a giant pair of men's feet, with longish toes sprouting pubic-looking hair and poking out of yoga dude brown leather Birkenstock sandals.

Somewhat eclipsed behind the soles of Sandalman's feet was an older guy in the center of the room, dressed in green pleated teacher pants—Dockers, maybe—and a white polo shirt with a black logo on it that said something I couldn't quite make out. Curved around and facing him were three others in addition to Sandalman, two girls and a guy. No one sat next to each other, empty chairs in between, and all had their backs to me, including Sandalman. There was no last row or corner of the room that I could drop myself into like high school, since everyone was in a semi-circle. With no open chairs on the ends, I was just going to have to squeeze in somewhere.

"You must be our newest group member," said the guy in the Dockers, smiling in a welcoming sort of way. "I'm Dr. Palmer, but everyone calls me Dr. Dan if that works for you," he said.

I nodded at him, my eyes bouncing around at the others who had now turned around, no doubt to get a look at the latest fuckup to join the crew.

"You're Jess, right?" asked Dr. Dan.

Still looking for a seat and thinking more that I should just get the hell out now, while I still could, I didn't answer.

"Jess, right?" Dr. Dan repeated.

"Oh, sorry, yes, I apologize. Jess, yes," I stammered, realizing

I might be coming across on the rude side by ignoring Dr. Dan long before he even asked me the Mac Daddy of therapy questions: *"How does that make you feel?"*

"Well, welcome, Jess, We are happy to have you. No apologies in here, by the way," he said, smiling again, like a grandparent who was always happy to see you.

"Hi, Jess. My name is Jacob and I'm an alcoholic," announced Sandalman, standing up and putting his hand on Dr. Dan's shoulder. Sandalman was really pasty white and sported quite the beard. It reminded me of late fall—browns and auburns and reds—all blending in and blanketing his face. A giant pile of leaves that needed to be raked, I thought.

"Hi, Jacob," the others responded in unison.

"Okay, cut it out," said Dr. Dan. "Jess, this is Jacob, but he is not an alcoholic. He is, however, recovering from a prescription drug addiction and is also a compulsive liar."

I couldn't tell if Dr. Dan was joking.

"As you can also see, Jacob could use a shower and a shave," Dr. Dan added.

"Hey, that's not fair, there, Dr. Dan," Sandalman said.

Again, I could not decipher whether these two were arguing or if it was something of a friendlier, and familiar, back-and-forth.

"I'm an irregular bather, Dr. Dan. A naturalist, some might call me," offered Sandalman.

"You're a big shit pile, that's what I would call you," said the skinny guy, two chairs to the right of Sandalman. He craned his neck to the side, exposing a protruding cheekbone and a long drawn-out nose. His face reminded me of something, but I couldn't, in that moment, decide what.

"Fuck you, Penis Face," said Sandalman.

That was it, I thought.

"All right, fellas," said Dr. Dan. "Jess, you met Jacob, and this is Dylan. Dylan has his own set of diagnoses, as you might have already surmised. Oppositional defiant disorder. Anger disorder, too. Right, Dylan?" Dr. Dan asked.

"Don't forget bipolar. I think I got that one, too," said Dylan, displaying a curious sense of pride.

"Could be," said Dr. Dan, nodding his head and turning to me. Jess, how about you find a seat?"

Penis Face, I mean Dylan, stood up and pulled out the empty chair, offering me the spot.

"Oh, thanks. That's okay. I'll sit over here," I said.

Certain that I did not want to sit between Sandalman and Penis Face, I took the open chair between the two girls in the room.

A delicate, Barbie doll–looking girl introduced herself from my left. She had a paperback book in her lap, holding her page with a freshly manicured finger. Everything about her was pretty; from the way she crossed her legs to how she smelled. Like a fresh bowl of fruit.

"It's a French," she said, removing her entire left hand from the book and flitting her manicured fingers for me to see. "I'm Kyra. Very happy to meet you," she said, extending her right hand as I sat down. "It will be good to have you to even things out," she said.

I must have looked confused.

"Men and women, she means," said the other girl. "With you, we will have three women, three men, not counting Dr. Dan over there, who probably hasn't gotten any pussy since 1980 or something like that. So we don't count him," she said.

"Really, Macy, the last time I got, I mean had sex, has nothing to do with our talk today," said Dr. Dan, clearly being politic, but not the least bit fazed.

"Well, now that we're on it, when was the last time you did get laid, Dr. Dan?" asked Penis Face.

Counting me, it looked to me like the women outnumbered the men, excluding Dr. Dan, the born-again virgin.

"It doesn't look like Kenny's going to make it today'" said Dr. Dan, ignoring the inquiry from Penis Face. "Let's get to it."

"Kenny's the karate guy," said Macy. "Just too funny. He wears his white karate suit, a 'gi' I think he calls it, whenever he shows up, which isn't too often. Bandana around his head and big white sneakers. Big doofus. Big doofus," Macy said.

"He's just autistic, is all," said Kyra, running those long French manicured nails through her hair.

"He is definitely on the Asperger's spectrum, Kyra, but I wouldn't say autistic. Plus, he is doing really well. He might still show up, but we are running behind, so we do need to keep things moving," Dr. Dan said, a little firmer this time.

"Why are you wearing long sleeves?" asked Penis Face, pointing at me. So much for working the new girl in slowly, I thought. "It's hot as balls out there," he said.

Rather than getting angry, which I think I had every right to do at the time, I laughed silently, thinking how a guy whose face looked like a penis was telling me that it was "hot as balls."

Before I could answer Penis Face, Macy slid into the chair next to me. There was something about her I immediately liked. Maybe it was how she looked, I thought. Macy was exotic, like no one I had ever seen before. Black, I thought, maybe Hispanic, maybe something else. Her skin was a buttery caramel. She wore torn boyfriend-style jeans and a black tank top that proclaimed "RAMONES RULE" in block lettering across her chest. Her green eyes arched when she looked at me and she ran her hand through a bouncy soft Afro kind of hairstyle.

"My parents are both white, real white, if you know what I mean," she offered, as if sensing I was trying to figure her out. "No hip-hop in my house, I can tell you that. They still play Barry Manilow records and watch PBS. Ever heard of Barry Manilow? Neil Diamond, too. You would not believe it," she said, taking a breath. "My adoptive parents, I mean. Can't say much about my biological parents. No clue. Think I was a crack baby, actually.

You know that Cher song, 'Half Breed'?"

I had heard of Cher, but didn't know the song. "No, don't know that one," I said.

"Well, I got so many different things running through me, when people ask, I don't tell them I'm white, black, or anything else. 'Sorta Rican' is how I see myself," she said.

"You two done yet?" asked Penis Face. "I think it's a fair question. I mean, she wants us to let her join in, and we have known each other for what, like two months now? Seems only fair that she should tell us why she is wearing long sleeves in the middle of a ninety-degree day," he said.

I got the distinct sense that Penis Face was egging me on for some reason that I could not understand, particularly since I had known him for all of maybe ten minutes.

Macy put her hand on my knee and leaned in, ignoring Penis Face. "I'll play it for you after group. 'Half Breed.' A little retro, but I do love Cher. The song, it's all me, no doubt. A half breed. Maybe I'm a quarter breed or eighth breed for all I know, but 'Half Breed' is the closest song I could find," she said.

Dr. Dan cut in. "Okay, Macy. We left off with you last week. You said that you were feeling, um, 'broken' is how you put it," he said.

"I don't really want to get into it, to be honest. Time has come and gone, I suppose," Macy said, trying to brush him away.

Clearly in control, Dr. Dan was not backing off. "Macy, that's not how we do things here. You know that. Everybody here has to do their part, share their part. This is your time. What's going on with you?" he asked.

Macy took her hand off my knee and sat back in her chair. She crossed her arms in front of her, pressing her breasts up into the scoop in her tank top. She didn't say a word.

Dr. Dan looked at her. Macy stared back, fearless and unmoving. Defiant. She opened her eyes wide, making her forehead crinkle, as if to say, *"Now what, motherfucker?"*

"I'm a cutter," I said, breaking the standoff and running interference for my new friend. "I stopped for a while, but my dad died and he was my best friend and he was gone and so I just did it."

I rambled on for a few more minutes. About my dad dying, my mom hating me, my sister wishing I were gone, my drinking, using pills, whatever came to mind. I had no idea what it was that got me spewing out the despair that my life had become. I just went on and on, like a ten-page single-spaced paragraph without punctuation. Also, though, I was talking to take the glare off of Macy, whom I knew just was not up for getting into the reasons for her being "broken."

"Thanks for sharing, Jess, and thanks from Macy I am sure for letting her off the hook, for now anyway. Does it make you feel better?" Dr. Dan asked.

"Does what make me feel better? The talking or the cutting?" I asked.

"Either. Both," said Dr. Dan.

"I guess so, yes," I said.

"I knew she was a cutter," said Penis Face. "No one wears long sleeves in this weather."

"Yeah, me too," sighed Kyra, looking up from her book.

"People cut for lots of reasons, you know," said Kyra, emitting a sense of understanding.

"Yeah, and what was the reason you jumped in front of that Metro bus, little miss expert?" asked Penis Face, boring his testicle eyes into Kyra.

Kyra shook her head. "We are trying to help Jess right now, Dylan," Kyra said, quite politely while putting her face back down into her book.

"So your dad died, and you're a cutter. Anything else we need to know?" asked Sandalman, running his fingers through the leaf pile.

"Well, I'm adopted, so there's that," I said.

"Oh, Jesus, you are fucked," said Penis Face, leaning back in his chair, clapping his hands together.

"I'm adopted, too," said Macy, leaning into me, just so our shoulders touched. Even though she had told me that just a couple minutes ago, I still appreciated it. I pressed back into her. Not in a sexual way. It was different. It was, like, in a friend way.

"No shit," said Penis Face. "I mean, look at you. You are one mixed-up pup," he said.

"Maybe that's why she feels broken," said Kyra, not looking up from her book. "I mean, Macy has no idea where all of her pieces came from," she said.

"You know, that is an excellent way of putting it," Dr. Dan said, standing up and grabbing his messenger bag from the back of his chair, just as a dude in a karate uniform walked in.

"You missed the whole session today, Kenny," Dr. Dan said.

"But I got my green belt," he responded, pointing to his waist.

"That's great," said Sandalman.

"HI-YA," screeched Penis Face, jumping into a karate stance.

"We all have a lot of pieces, some missing, some maybe broken," Dr. Dan said, patting my shoulder as he walked past me and out the door.

That's for fucking sure, I thought.

TWENTY-ONE

JB

With our kids grown and no longer looking to us for much of anything other than some money and an occasional Sunday night dinner, Laurie was looking for new ways to keep me occupied, get me feeling good about myself. Probably not quite as bad as keeping a bored four-year-old busy in a restaurant, but close. She tried just about anything. I could teach. Work evenings at a bar. Join a motorcycle club. Something to curb my moping.

"Why don't you try to write that book you've been talking about?" she asked me, just a few hours after I had spoken with Jess.

"Waste of time," I answered. "Who's going to read something written by a fifty-three-year-old divorce lawyer who wishes he were something else?"

"I would," she answered. "Maybe if it was any good, a lot of people would read it. You never know," she said.

"Nah. Doubt that, but thanks. Don't worry, I'll figure it out," I said.

"Well, you need to do something. I know you are tired of your job, but we still need you to work. And you need to either find something to plug into at the job or at least do something when you get home other than talk to the dog," she said.

"He's a good listener. And at least he wags his tail when I walk in the door," I said, patting the top of Shane's head. His tail thumped on the floor, on cue.

"Well I'll wag mine for you if that's all it takes," Laurie said, shaking her ass in front of the kitchen sink. "But you still need to do something. This moping around the house thing has got to stop. I mean, I love you, but it's driving me nuts. I can hear you sighing seventeen times a day," she said.

"I talked to Jess today," I said, figuring this could be my

73

chance to throw out the idea of my heading to Florida for a few days.

"Tom's girl?" Laurie asked, knowing the answer. "Sweet kid. Last I heard when I ran into Lianne was that she had left, moved away."

"Well, she's in Florida. Lianne called me to make sure she would be up here for the unveiling next month and when I was on the phone about that, Jess asked me to help her out with something. Wanted me to help her find her biological parents," I said.

"So, are you going to do it? Help her?" Laurie asked.

"I think I will, yeah," I said, petting the dog again. "Actually, I thought I would go down there for a few days. To Florida. Get away, talk to Jess, go over what we can do, see if she is really up for it," I told her.

I thought for sure Laurie would ask me why I needed to go to Florida when it was easier to just talk to Jess on the phone, email or Skype with her. She would be right. There was no reason I had to get on a plane, fly two and a half hours, and sit on a beach to help Jess find her birth family. I looked away, waiting and, yes, sighing.

"You should do it," she said.

TWENTY-TWO

Jess

In the weeks after we met, Macy and I spent a lot of time together. We met at the local Safeway in the mornings and had coffee in the Starbucks inside the store. There was another freestanding coffee shop just around the corner, but Macy said she did not like to go to that one because of the good chance we would see someone she knew from high school.

Like me, Macy didn't have a yearbook filled with the purple-penned notes from kids you probably will never see again, reminding her of the "fun times" they spent together in high school and promising to "stay in touch" after graduation. Not black, not white and certainly not a down the middle of the road type, Macy never found that place, or space, within which she could make friends and navigate high school life.

While we sipped our Frappuccinos or caramel lattes, extra whip, Macy told me stories of locker room fights with girls, shouting matches in classrooms, and several one- or two-day school suspensions. While I was somehow able to eke my way through school and get my diploma, Macy was ultimately tossed from school and had to finish her senior year in the county's "home and hospital" care program.

"I remember the school psychologist meeting with us and saying, 'Oh, not to worry, Mr. and Mrs. Meeks, Macy will be fine. The county pays for interim instructional services. It's for students just like Macy here, who are unable to attend a regular program, like most kids, due to a mental or physical condition,'" Macy said, scrunching her lips in what I supposed was an imitation of the county employee who gave her parents the news.

"Since I knew I looked good, I mean boys always were talking to me about hooking up and all that, it must have been that I had some sort of mental condition. It didn't matter to me, really. Even the parts about me not being like most kids. I was fine with it," she said.

I wasn't sure I believed her, but I nodded my head anyway. All that shit I went through, well, it did bother me. It was hard for me to believe she was okay with being taken out of school, no matter how bad things were for her there.

"Anyway," Macy went on, "I called it home schooling, because that sounded cool to me. Like those Mormons in Utah or Amish people who get to stay home and not go to school. Plus, I got to sleep late, the teacher, or whatever she was, maybe showed up half the times she was supposed to and I never even had to take a test. I got a report card, all Cs, and they sent me my diploma a month or so later," she said.

Macy was still living with her parents, no more than ten minutes from where I grew up. It turned out that we even went to the all the same schools, but Macy was a couple of years older and we had never met. Thinking of her living so close reminded me of those old photos people sometimes find where two little kids who didn't know each other but are standing close enough to be in the same picture years later become friends or even get married.

One morning at our usual spot, a bench next to where the barista made all the drinks behind the counter, Macy told me she was leaving. It was like someone ran over my puppy. I cried. Even though we had only known each other a short time, I just knew that Macy and I were destined to be friends for life, connected somehow by the uncertain bonds of adoption, of rejection, of hurt and more. How could she leave me? Just like that? The tears streamed down my cheeks, splashing into my coffee, staining the white cardboard cup.

"Jesus Christ, come on, girl. You don't understand," Macy said, resting her hand on my shoulder. "You need to come, too. My cousin Bobby, he runs this restaurant bar place down in Florida, right on the beach. We saw each other a lot when we were little, but when his parents got divorced, he moved with his mom to Florida. I found him a couple months ago on Facebook," she said.

By this time, I was doing that little girl troubled breathing kind of cry, making a deep yelping sound between breaths and sniffles. I didn't even care when my nose dripped onto the last puff of whipped cream.

"You need to stop, Jess, girl. Listen to me. Bobby, he sent me a Facebook message a couple of weeks ago, told me I should come visit, work at his bar even. Said there was a couple of teeny apartments right down the road, a block from the beach, just one room and a bathroom, but shit, almost on the beach. They need some people to work and I need to get out of this town," she said.

"I hope you're not mad, and you can say no if you want, but I told him I was coming and a friend, too. He's counting on us, so you need to come. We can live next to each other; it'll be like college, but without the classes. We'll be our own sorority."

I wiped my cheeks and caught my breath. I could tell she had thought this all out.

"So?" she asked, looking at me with those Siamese cat green eyes, her head cocked to one side.

Like most people faced with an unexpected opportunity to completely change their lives, my first inclination was to say no, I couldn't do it. I couldn't leave my minimum wage job at the Uptown Cheapskate where I sold stained and sometimes decomposing second- or third-hand clothes and had to hold my breath whenever I went into the place for like a minute until I could get used its musty, old attic smell. I couldn't leave my bed, my room, my house. I couldn't leave my family, what was left of it, with my dad gone, even though I had not spoken with my mom in a week and I knew my sister felt the same about me as I did about her. A thousand miles from home? I wasn't happy, no, but I was comfortable, I knew what to expect. I had a routine. Leave and go to a place I had never been? I couldn't do it. No way, I thought.

I grabbed Macy's hand and squeezed. I looked right back at her.

"I'm in," I said.

TWENTY-THREE

JB

Laurie makes fun of me before every trip we take together. For close to a week before we leave, I turn into a poster child for someone with obsessive compulsive disorder. I like to talk about what she is packing; what I should bring with me. Do I need anything dressier than a T-shirt for when we go out? How many pairs of jeans? Which shoes? In the days before the trip, I will stack my provisions into piles, just to be sure I can see everything before it goes into the suitcase. Socks, underwear. Dwelling. Extra contact lenses. Mulling. And, what about hats? Which ones? How should I pack them so they don't get crushed? Laurie, to her credit, generally says nothing. She smiles, looks at my two weeks' worth of clothes set aside for what is only a three- or four-day trip and makes not a comment, knowing that no matter how far in advance I plan and how much I try to be sure I am completely organized and ready, I will, without fail, forget something.

* * *

Although my piles of supplies were ready to be packed, I first had to spend a couple of days in trial over what had become known in my office as "the deaf lesbian dog lover case." Seven or eight months ago, Karen Dyson, a deaf professor at Gallaudet University, came to see me and told me that she and her partner, Bonnie Vincent, also a professor at Gallaudet had recently broken up after seven years of living together. Since I could not sign, Karen brought her brother with her, who translated things for me. As traumatic as the breakup was, with her partner packing up and emptying out the house one afternoon while Karen was at work, it was made even more distressing because she took Karen's dog, Chowder. According to Karen, Chowder had been a gift to her from a woman nearby, whose dog had puppies.

"Is Chowder an expensive dog? What breed?" I asked, forgetting that I was only supposed to ask one question at a time before moving to the next.

Karen shook her head and signed.

"No. He's not expensive. He's not any breed," Karen's brother translated.

I had heard of dogs trained to help people who were hearing impaired, alerting them to different sounds in the house, when a phone or doorbell rang. "Is he an assistance dog?" I asked.

Karen must have been reading my lips. She was shaking her head before I finished my sentence.

"No, he's not trained to do anything," her brother said, shaking his head.

Chowder was just a mutt. A mutt that Karen loved and wanted back. I get it, I thought.

After Karen hired me, I immediately filed what is called a replevin case against Karen's former partner, asking that a judge in the District Court, considered the lower trial court in Maryland, order Chowder's return to his rightful owner. We had a short trial a couple of months later and after taking testimony from both parties and a couple of witnesses, a District Court judge agreed with us and ordered that Chowder should be returned to Karen.

Figuring that was that, I closed my file, wished Karen good luck and went back to fighting over kids and money, rather than dogs. Unfortunately, in Maryland, many types of cases that are heard in the District Court can be appealed and heard all over again, "de novo" it is called, in the upper trial court, which is called the Circuit Court. Damned if Bonnie didn't note her appeal, forcing us to again go to trial over Chowder, a shepherd-collie-beagle—who knows what mix—with no particular talents.

The lawyer on the other side, Scott Silver, was a decent, hardworking guy. In private, quietly in a hallway or in the men's room, we joked about the case, eventually eliminating the conversation and instead greeting each other with a bark or two. Since he knew that I could make a strong case for keeping Chowder with my client, Scott took a different tact. He basically turned the trial into a divorce case, offering witness after witness to testify about the relationship between Bonnie and Karen, how difficult Karen could be, that Bonnie was justified in leaving and so on. Of course, none of this had anything to do what the case was really about—who owned little or actually medium-sized Chowder. But for whatever reason, either because it was easy—no real legal milestones or precedents coming from this one—or maybe because he was enjoying the spectacle of it all, our judge, a former state prosecutor, Eric Robinson, overruled every single one of my objections, let the witnesses testify, and let the case go on—for nearly three days.

By the end of the first day, the small courtroom that we were assigned to had swelled with observers to such an extent that people were lining the walls. When I used to dream of trying a case in front of a standing room only crowd, the dream involved some huge celebrity-laden, media circus thing. Not a knockdown, drag-out over a thirty-five pound pooch.

On day three, the clerk moved us to the large ceremonial courtroom, usually set aside for media interest cases or much grander proceedings, like year-end memorials to lawyers who had died during the past twelve months.

Worse than the gallery itself was the temperament of those in it. Made up of entirely hearing-impaired gay women, everyone seemed to have chosen a side, with Bonnie's friends on one side of the aisle and Karen's behind our trial table on the other. The judge brought in three deaf interpreters, so that everyone throughout the courtroom could follow the testimony and goings-on of the trial. Later, I found out that the case had developed an underground following among the courthouse employees, many of whom watched the closed circuit feed during their breaks.

Bonnie's friends were particularly vociferous whenever I stood up, howling and grunting in that guttural way that some hearing-impaired people do when they are trying to speak. As a group, they sounded eerily like seals or otters or some such thing and every time it happened, Judge Robinson would tell them to be quiet and threaten to empty the courtroom. I wasn't sure why these people hated my client or me, nor did I care, since, after all, my job was simple—to make sure Chowder lived out the rest of his doggie days with Karen.

Sometime during the first day was when I heard the first squawk of *"Beh-kuh"* from Bonnie's side of the gallery. I looked back reflexively to see a heavyset, Romanian-wrestler-like woman with hearing aids in both ears and an "I'm going to fuck you up" look on her face, pointing at me. I stared for a minute, and then, in a moment of immaturity for which I remain infinitely proud of myself, blew a silent raspberry her way before turning back to face the bench and Judge Robinson.

At close to 3:00 pm on the third day of Bonnie's case, my friend Scott finished and rested his case. I immediately made an oral motion to dismiss the case, arguing that Bonnie had not once in three days and through eighteen witnesses put forth any evidence whatsoever that she was the owner of the dog. There was testimony that she helped to take care of the dog, feed the dog, and God knows she loved the dog. Nothing, however as to the real issue, the real reason we were there burning up tens of thousands of tax dollars for a good part of the week—that she owned Chowder. It was an easy call, I thought. I made what I thought was a compelling argument and asked Judge Robinson to dismiss the case and allow my client to live her life in peace with Chowder.

Judge Robinson denied the motion.

"Mr. Becker, I assume you will need some time for your case, so maybe we should recess for the rest of the day and start back up tomorrow morning," Judge Robinson, unzipping his robe a bit just under his neck.

"How much time will you need to put on your client's case?" he asked me.

"Five minutes," I said.

He zipped the robe back up. "Let's get to it then, Mr. Becker. I will give you your five minutes and just five minutes," smirking at me as if to say, *No lawyer does anything in five minutes, smart ass.*

I called my one and only witness.

"Ma'am, please state your name and address for the record."

"Robin Chambers. I live at 433 Wyndham Terrace, Washington DC."

Robin just looked like a dog person. Her graying hair was all fluffy on one side and flat on the other, as if she gave a no more than a glancing attempt to comb it at the last minute before leaving the house. She wore an ankle-length wool skirt with gray flat shoes and a burgundy blouse that had just the slightest outlines of some sort of stain on her left shoulder.

"Ms. Chambers, do you have a dog?"

"Yes. Two. A male and a female."

"What are your dogs' names?"

"Boston is the male. Soupy is the girl."

"Did there come a time when Soupy had puppies?"

"Yes. Before Boston was snipped—neutered—he and Soupy apparently had a little late-night rendezvous in our basement. Soupy had four puppies, three males and one female."

"What did you do with the puppies?"

"Well, you can't really sell a bunch of mutts, so I figured I would give them to some friends."

"Were you friendly with either of the parties in this case before the puppies were born?"

"Yes. Karen Dyson and I have been close friends since she moved to DC for college."

After asking the Court's permission, I approached the witness stand and showed her a picture of Chowder.

"Do you recognize this dog, Ms. Chambers?"

"I sure do. That's sweet Chowder. Such a baby." She looked at the picture as if it were her six-year-old son taking his first bike ride without training wheels.

"Was Chowder one of Soupy's puppies?"

Four years of college, three years of law school, and a summer of studying for the bar exam so that I could get straight the lineage of this litter of puppies, I thought to myself.

"Sure was."

"Did you give Chowder away?"

"Yes, I did."

And who did you give Chowder to?"

She smiled our way and pointed to my left. "To Karen Dyson," she said.

"Thank you, Ms. Chambers."

I took a long and purposefully obvious look at my watch and then up at Judge Robinson.

Four minutes. Time to spare.

"No further questions, Your Honor. That's our case," I said.

* * *

After a brief closing argument, Judge Robinson entered judgment and awarded ownership of Chowder, "now and forever, thank God," as he put it, to my client. As I packed up my case, Karen gave me a hug and was then immediately swallowed into a sea of happy and teary-eyed deaf lesbians.

Out in the hallway, I was greeted by the remaining hangers-on from Bonnie's side of the room, with several pairs of eyes bulging and glaring at me. A last chorus of *"Beh-kuh, Beh-kuh"* barked and bellowed behind me as I made my way through the hallway. Happily dropping my lawyer facade for the guy I really prefer to be, I shot them the finger as the elevator door closed.

TWENTY-FOUR

Jess

Macy left a couple of days later, but I had to give my two weeks' notice at work and tell my mother about my leaving. It wasn't hard to do. Not that I was surprised, but it did make me sad. A little.

"Mom," I said, in the kitchen. "I need to talk to you about something." Still as rigid as she was when I was growing up, my mother compulsively stuck to her daily routine and it was therefore pretty easy to steer clear of her. Like a clock, she was up at seven. As it was every morning since she started working out soon after my dad died, she was at her computer in some black yoga pants and a bright pink, low cut, racer-style tank top from the Lululemon store. Funny, I couldn't remember her ever wearing a tank top before, but I don't know, whatever, I thought.

When I spoke, she didn't turn from her computer, instead continuing to get her daily news online. From Facebook.

We used to get the *Washington Post* delivered to our house every morning. My father read the sports page in the mornings, and then left the rest for when he got home from work in the afternoon. A stickler for making sure everything was in its place, my mother hated seeing the paper on the kitchen table all day so she would sometimes toss it in the recycling or, even worse, stuff it in the trash can out in the garage. That was the one thing I can remember that pissed my father off, as he could never under-stand the big problem my mom had with a newspaper sitting on top of the kitchen table for a few hours, not to mention his having to go rummage through the trash to find it. Like anything else as I grew up, if something upset my dad, it upset me, even though I didn't much read the paper either. Soon after my dad died, my mom cancelled the subscription.

I tried again. "Mom, if you have a minute. I want you to know

I am leaving."

She picked up her green tea and sipped, not moving.

"I'm moving to Florida with Macy. I think I need a change. I hope you understand," I said.

She turned, just slightly, in my direction and nodded her head, barely looking at me. "Figures," was all she said, before going back to the latest *"you really need to see this—OMG!"* Facebook video on her computer screen.

"Okay, well I'm not trying to fight. I just need to go. You've got Kasey anyway," I said, standing my ground and talking to her bare shoulders. Hoping, I guess, that she would get up and hug me. Tell me she loved me. Ask me to stay.

"Do what suits you. You will anyway," she said, before queuing up the video, something about a dog alone on a glacier being saved by Russian fishermen.

* * *

I didn't say anything. I didn't know what to say. I waited, still hoping for a "Good luck, Jess. I love you." *Maybe that hug,* I thought. She did neither.

I packed up and left the next day.

I haven't talked to her since.

TWENTY-FIVE

Jess

Jacked up on Adderall and Juicy Fruits, I carved right through the mid-Atlantic and southeastern states. Stopping only to pee and mix up Diet Coke and five-hour energy cocktails, I hit my exit, Donald Ross Road, in just about fifteen hours. I had no idea who Donald Ross was but decided right then I would find out.

From there it was due east toward the ocean and Jones Beach and whatever was there to help me get my awesome back. The sun was just rising, pink and pretty through some wispy clouds, as I sped toward it, thinking of what I had left behind, my mom and sister, my job, my life. Maybe I cried for a second or two as I crossed over a little bridge and the Inner Coastal Waterway. I played with the radio and found Fleetwood Mac's "Go Your Own Way," continuing straight ahead to the dead end that Macy told me about and right onto Ocean Road, through Juno Beach.

Juno was really pretty, with homes that looked like they came from Spain or maybe Mexico, made of stucco, with bronze and copper roofs and windows everywhere. Many of them had gated driveways. Looking at all the expensive places that people lived, or maybe just spent their winters, escaping from Boston or New York or wherever, those gates struck me funny, as I looked around and wondered whom exactly the gates were supposed to keep out. Other people with gated driveways?

I laughed and kept going, a few runners and people on their bikes were on either side of the road. I passed fancy high-rises with names like "The Beachfront," "The Waterfront," and "The Horizon." It was hard for me to believe that I was going to live in one of these kinds of places, on the beach looking out at the ocean every day. Maybe I would get me a nice high-back wicker chair for my patio, like the ones you see in island pictures on the Internet, to sit and have coffee in the mornings, margaritas at night. A nice ocean breeze would blow through and I would shake my hair off my face and pull it back into a ponytail. Me, in a ponytail? No way, I thought. But I was starting new and I did have this porch and the wicker chair and the coffee and, oh man, I was so excited.

Some sun-drenched white-haired kid on a Razor scooter slapped the hood of my car.

"Come on, already. You going or what, lady?" he hollered from my left, next to the stop sign.

He had a tan that looked like it would be long into the next decade before it faded and stared at me through sunglasses with those frames that bend around your forehead to keep out the glare.

"Shit, sorry," I said, although he probably didn't hear me. I punched the gas, and bent around to the left, off Ocean Road and onto Sandcastle Way, passing a dingy *T*-shaped wooden sign that read "*JONE EACH*" and had what looked to be a salmon-colored turtle painted under the *H*. Immediately, my dreams of a beach-front paradise condo washed out with the morning's tide. Jones Beach was not Juno Beach. No high-rise buildings, no European architecture. No gates.

At first, there weren't any houses or buildings at all and the grass on either side of the road was not cut. What I thought were tall weeds being whipped back and forth in the breeze, I later learned were really "quack grass." I laughed, thinking that maybe the name came from after the regulars at The Shipwreck.

I checked my note with the address that Macy had given me just to be sure I was in the right place, or near it anyway.

The Paradise Cove apartments were out of place. They looked more like they belonged in west Baltimore, not in Florida. The building was a small cement structure with eight doors, four upstairs and four down, all of which were peeling and flaking and needing paint. Long windows covered by faded blue awnings were next to each door and served to divide the apartments. Rusty lattice-looking fencing closed in the outdoor walkway on both levels and there was a stairway on either side of the building, like the ones they have on roadside motels in old black-and-white movies, just in case I thought someone got murdered and the killer needed to get away quickly.

I parked across the street, in front of a woman in a thick buttoned-up green sweater doing nothing but sitting on a wooden bench, looking oblivious to the fact that it was on only three good legs, with the fourth propped but sinking on mounds of cardboard.

Not exactly the start to getting that awesome thing back, I thought, grabbing my small duffel and getting out of the car.

As I walked toward the apartments, still a little wobbly from the ride down the East Coast, a dark-haired guy came out of one of the upstairs apartments, wearing jeans and a wife beater. A mound of salt-and-pepper bedhead stuck out every which way as he looked down at me and lit a cigarette.

"You must be Jess," he said, blowing smoke down my direction and clearing his throat.

I went to answer, trying not to notice that his jeans were not all the way buttoned. I always loved those button fly jeans on guys. They were sexier than a zipper. Even on this guy, who was definitely much older than me.

"You speak?" he asked, as I had neglected to answer his first question, lost in the guy's Levi's.

"Oh, yeah, sorry," I said, cocking my head and doing my best to look pretty.

Before I could say anything else, button-fly guy was walking down the hallway and banging on his neighbor's door. "Mace, your friend's here," he said, way too loud for seven in the morning.

I heard a squeal from inside the apartment. Button-fly guy looked back at me and ran his hand through his hair, the cigarette dangling out from between his lips. "Nice meeting you. See you at work," he said, going back into his apartment.

Watching Macy bound out of her apartment and down the stairs, her soft curly hair bouncing with each step, I felt so happy. Someone was happy to see me. Me.

"So, you met Bobby," Macy said, wrapping her arms around me. "He's great. God, I'm so glad you made it, girl." She really meant it. I don't think I had gotten a hug like that, a real arms around, squeeze me tight hug, since my dad died.

I hugged her back. I was a little curious and, yes, interested. "I thought you said Bobby was your cousin?" I asked.

"It's like your dad's friend you call 'uncle,' you know, Bobby is not really a cousin, but our families were close growing up, so we think of each other like cousins. He's older than me, so actually more like an uncle, I guess," Macy said, not letting me go.

"He runs The Shipwreck?" I asked.

Macy pulled back, grinning at me, having already noticed that I had noticed. "Girl," she said, "he's old enough to be your daddy. But yes, he runs the bar. He is also the building manager here at The Cove. Your place is directly under his. Only a jump down the stairs from me, too," she said, gleaming.

"Cool," I said, feeling particularly pleased with myself and holding Macy's hand as she took me in to show me my new place.

TWENTY-SIX

Jess

Thankfully, there was not a lot of time for me to think about all that I had left behind, or rather, the little I had left behind, by coming here. I missed my dad, but of course, I missed him when I was home too. One reason I decided to leave Maryland was that I was absolutely sure that it would be easier on me not to be at home. Not to see my mom sitting in his chair at the kitchen table and somehow thinking that just wasn't right. Not going past his office in the front of the house, where he paid bills, looked at Maryland basketball news on his computer, and kept his autographed Springsteen guitar on a stand in the corner. Not to every day walk past the hallway full of family pictures, all fading and yellow from the sunlight that poured in through the oval window in the front of the house.

As it turns out, though, I seem to think about him more since I have been here. Down the street from my apartment, there's a little playground tucked into a grassy area with a nest of always bending palm trees. The area isn't unusual or out of the ordinary. A run-of-the-mill jungle gym sits on a wide bed of wood chip mulch stuff and there is a blacktop with a basketball hoop on one side. The hoop has a rusty metal net that makes an old cash register swooshy kind of sound whenever a kid makes a basket.

I like to walk over there sometimes, and when I do it seems this little girl is always there with her dad. I sit on the bench with my sunglasses on, shading me from the sun, but also hiding the fact that I am watching those two and the game that the dad plays with his little girl. He pushes the swing, just barely at first and she laughs.

"No, daddy. Higher and higher," she says.

"Okay, but you got to put some more money in the machine," he says back, putting his two hands out around her sides from behind the swing.

The little girl slaps his hands, pretending to put more money in. "There's two more quarters. Higher and higher, please." She draws out the *"pleeease"* and begs, a big, baby-toothed smile, shining white.

This goes on and on, and for some reason, I feel like I could watch forever. More change in her daddy's pretend machine, the higher the girl goes, her blonde curls flying with every giggle and push of the swing. The first time I saw them, right out of nowhere, I cried. Now, though, after sitting and watching these two, I don't know how many times since I have been here, there is something about seeing them that feels right, somehow comforted. Connected, maybe. I am that little girl on the swing, my dad tickling me from behind with every push, as I kick my legs, zooming into the sky. I take a breath and turn away from the dad and the little blonde-haired girl. I don't want to look at those two anymore. I don't want to hear them.

That's not me. My dad left me. He's gone.

TWENTY-SEVEN

Jess

I surprised myself a little by not just throwing all my stuff in the closet and leaving the apartment as it was when I moved in. Since it came furnished, mostly with what clearly was passed-down stuff from a college dorm room, I could have left the place as is, other than plug in my coffeemaker and fix up the bathroom, always my favorite room ever since I was little. Instead, I spent the first two or three days driving around to secondhand stores and a huge Goodwill shop up north in Jupiter. I found a neat rocking chair for thirty bucks and a couple of cool beach kind of prints for the walls, two for six dollars. The pictures were colorful and funky and not like the ones that you see in some pretentious people's beach houses. The walls were a boring off-white color, and I wasn't allowed to paint so I just hung the prints up in the main room, thinking it was better to make that area decent in case I ever had any friends over. My bedroom I left pretty barren, with just a queen-size bed, dresser, and nightstand. I got rid of the yucky light blue sheets and pilled-up brown blanket, replacing them with some bedding I brought from home. The dresser and nightstand were both beige and looked kind of like wood, but felt and smelled like plastic. The top two drawers in the dresser stuck and were tricky to open. The one on the bottom slid open if I pulled hard, but it was held together with packing tape. On the nightstand was a brass-like lamp that was peeling on its base and worked when it wanted to, which rarely was at night.

Most everyone who lived at The Cove also worked at the bar. There was Cary, a grungy, hippie who moved down from West Virginia and now worked the grill at The Shipwreck, every day wearing one of those leather Aussie outback hats with the string hanging under his chin when he rode his bike to work, even in the sweaty Florida summer. In the other unit upstairs between

Macy and Cary was another guy whom everyone called "Seeds," either because he was from Nebraska or possibly due to the sesame-looking pimples that dotted his face. Seeds stayed in back and washed dishes at The Wreck, because Bobby was afraid that the dude's acne would scare customers away.

My unit was on the first floor and despite the planned "sorority," Macy and I didn't see each other all that much outside The Wreck. We worked crazy hours; the *B* shift as Bobby called it, as in "be there when it opens and be there when it closes." That meant noon until two in the morning on weekdays and eleven to three am on weekends. After work, we usually stayed for an hour or so, knocking back cold beers and tequila or whiskey shots or whatever Bobby was okay with us siphoning from the bar's overstock shelf. Mornings and usually early afternoons were spent sleeping at home, sleeping on the beach, and for me, every so often anyway, fucking.

TWENTY-EIGHT

JB

Thirty thousand feet up and my litigator's contribution to the American Kennel Club behind me, I tried unsuccessfully to nap on the plane. I was able to snag one of those front row seats so that although there was no tray or place to keep a bag, I had plenty of room to stretch out. I took the aisle spot to avoid climbing over anyone when I had to go to the bathroom, which was likely to happen probably twice over a two and a half hour flight. With all the commercials and ads about men who had to pee too so much because of enlarged prostates, I sometimes worried that, in my mid-fifties, I was on borrowed time. The fact was, however, that I was a frequent pisser for as long as I could remember. I had better things to worry about, including the increasingly apparent fragile state of my mental health.

Like the whole gluten-free wave, peanut allergies seemed to have overtaken much of the general population in such force that even if there is one person on an airplane who is allergic, the rest of us are stuck gnawing on those stale and tasteless airline crackers that come eight to a bag. Washing mine down with a Diet Coke, I found myself not thinking so much of Jess and how I was helping her, but more about me and what exactly it was I was trying to accomplish. Sure, I had information for her and it looked like we knew who her biological mother was, where she lived. A phone call or two and maybe Jess would have her answer, an answer to whatever the question was that got her focused on finding the woman in the first place.

As for me, I had my own questions. What is it I am searching for? Why was I even on this plane?

TWENTY-NINE

Jess

I knew it was nuts, but I really wanted to sleep with Bobby. Even though Macy said she thought he was close to fifty, more than twice my age, plus he had that "uncle" thing going on with her, none of that bothered me and, in fact, I liked it. I did my best to get him to notice me, sometimes heading on to the grass out front of The Cove in my boxers and barely there cropped pink tank top, pretending I was taking in some sun or just thinking to myself. Of course, I was really hoping he would look down at me from the balcony above, where he always seemed to stand, staring out at the lake or pond or whatever it was, with The Shipwreck across on the other side.

At work, my first week was spent with Bobby training me to bartend. In what I was sure was a well-thought-out marketing plan, there were no male bartenders at The Wreck and all of us girls wore the required baby doll Shipwreck tee, black during the week, close to see-through white on Saturday nights, climb up your crotch khaki shorts. and low-top black Converse sneakers. They also made us put this sheeny kind of stuff on our legs, Nivea Shimmer. Of the whole "don't you want me, baby" looking outfit, the shoes actually bothered me the most, because after eight or ten hours of working the bar in those things, my feet ached like shit.

I played that get-up for all it was worth trying to get Bobby's attention—bending here, stretching there, anything I could think of, but he didn't seem to notice anything other than to be sure I was getting the bartending thing down. Cleaning bar glasses was a simple science, dunking, and then dunking again, and then rinsing, right to left in the three-compartment sink. I learned how to free pour and count off a one-ounce shot and, of course, which drinks to shake—sours, drinks with juices—and which ones to stir—martinis and the like. Bobby warned me about the jerk-offs that would come in and tell me to stir things that were supposed to be shaken, complaining that shaking the booze would somehow "bruise" it.

"It's bullshit. Alcohol doesn't bruise, arms do," he said, "but just go with it. It's only the guys with money that will ask, so do what they want. You get a nice tip; we make more money for the up charge. Everyone's happy."

Although it was old and at some point, I don't know how long ago, The Shipwreck had probably seen better days, there was definitely a certain vibe to the place that was kind of cool. But for the two-piece SHIPWRECK sign out front (the word *ship* on one piece and *wreck* on the other) and gravel parking lots on either side, it could have easily been mistaken for one of the many other run-down, weather-washed bungalows that dotted Jones Beach.

As if to make sure customers knew right away they were not stepping into a restaurant, the bar was massive and oval shaped, dark wood, aging and grainy, but polished and clean, occupying almost the entirety of the place. It was surrounded by large wooden stools, with leather backs to keep the drinkers comfortable, and hanging above were all sorts of pieces I guess you would find in a real shipwreck—ropes, a couple of rudders and wood planks, as well as two steering wheels. More than once during my first few week working I was reminded that on a boat, it's not really a steering wheel, it's called a "helm." Not that I really gave a shit, but sure, okay, it was a helm.

In the center, where all the bartenders could reach, was a bell that Bobby said came from a boat called the *Lofthus*, a Norwegian trade ship that sank off the coast of Boynton Beach a little ways south of here, back in 1898. To me, it looked more like a fake bell that you could buy from some collector, or even at a HomeGoods store, but the bell was big and it really worked. The bell got rung for any number of things—a good tip, some guy buying a round of shots for girls on the other side of the bar, and, at just the right time of night, to make sure everyone squeezed onto the wood plank dance floor or sang along to an old classic song, like Neil Diamond's "Sweet Caroline" or The Four Seasons' "I Can't Take My Eyes off of You."

Country was also big at The Wreck, so guys like Luke Bryan and Brad Paisley got a lot of spin, along with Carrie Underwood and Miranda Lambert. Although not generally a fan of ladies' nights, it was a good moneymaker for us and since The Wreck was a place with never ending traditions, Thursdays at eleven meant free shots for all women who would jump on the dance floor and strip off at least one item of clothing to Joe Nichols's "Tequila Makes Her Clothes Fall Off."

It didn't take too much of Bobby's training to serve most of The Wreck's regulars. Steve and Kip, two clean-cut guys who used to be in the Coast Guard and now worked part time at a local bike place in Juno, had permanent seats to the left of the beer taps and across from the only high-definition TV in The Wreck. They were both muscular and good-looking, with haircuts "high and tight," they called them, from weekly trips to a local barbershop next to the bike store. I liked Kip maybe a bit more; while Steve often seemed to be scanning the place during timeouts and commercial breaks of whatever game was on, Kip was one of those guys that actually looked at you when you talked and, unless he was one hell of an actor, seemed sincerely interested in me. It was a little bit hard getting past his obsessive-compulsive gum cracking whenever we talked, but I liked Kip.

"What's with the gum?" I asked him.

"Gum is like, I think, man's greatest invention," he said. "I mean, it keeps me from eating one of those greasy burgers that Cary grills up, plus it keeps my breath fresh just in case, you know, some little pretty wants to get close and all that."

I looked at him and wondered if he thought I qualified as a "little pretty."

Katie, a tall and gangly redheaded girl who wore hipster black horned-rim glasses making it look like she just finished her day at the local library, showed up most nights after she got off work waiting tables at a high-end steakhouse down in Palm Beach Gardens, a couple of miles to the south. She would plunk herself down between Kip and Steve, draping her arms around both like you would a comfy couch. Like most of the locals, they generally stuck with beers and simple stuff like vodka sodas, Captain and Cokes, and margaritas.

The real money was made from running the charge cards of the "Downies," as we called them. Those were usually kids my age that lived nearby, downtown West Palm or around there, but not in Jones, mostly out of college and in their first jobs. The Downies filled the place most Saturdays and Thursdays for half-price ladies' nights, looking to dance, drink cheap, and hopefully get laid.

Although they annoyed the hell out of the regular folks, not to mention all of us who worked there, we learned very quickly, mostly from Bobby, that The Wreck needed the Downies' business and therefore, if we wanted to keep working, not to mention living in The Cove, we needed to treat them right. Most of my training time, consequently, was spent learning to make the drinks those crackers wanted to drink. Just like in life, a "blonde-headed slut" was pretty much the same as a "redheaded slut," except the Jaeger and peach schnapps were mixed with pineapple instead of cranberry. Those fucking people loved their peach schnapps. Between the two sluts and shots of "silk panties," another peach schnapps drink but shaken with vodka, we must have gone through a dozen or so bottles of the stuff every Saturday night.

THIRTY

Jess

With my dad's friend, my Uncle Bro, coming down in a day or two, I was feeling uneasy, shaky somehow. After we closed down the bar one Saturday night, a couple of days before he was supposed to show up, I just knew I was not going to be able to sleep. With another quiet Sunday morning just hours away, I found Kip outside in the parking lot making sure Katie was okay to drive, sipping a bottle of Miller High Life and, as usual, cracking his gum like a rubber band.

"Hey, Jess. Good night tonight, huh?" Kip said, more making a statement than asking a question. *Crack, crack.*

"Yeah, not bad. Got coffee money for the morning, so all is good," I answered, smiling a little longer at him than I normally would have done had I not banged back three shots of Jack while I was wiping down the bar.

"You want to come over and hang out a bit?" I asked him.

"You sure?" he asked back. Two more cracks.

"Wouldn't have asked if I wasn't sure," I said, grabbing his beer.

I took the last sip and handed him back the empty bottle. He smiled and tossed the bottle into the dumpster, clanging like the bell inside The Wreck.

"Sure, then. Let's go," he said, squeezing my hand. Tight.

Crack, crack, crack.

* * *

Kip was peeling off my shorts before I could close the door. As we both struggled to yank my shirt over my head, I remembered that I had been at work for twelve hours and was coated in a sticky batter of beer, grease, and sweat. I did not smell good. No normal human would have wanted to be near me. A horny guy with a hard-on, of course, doesn't worry too much about how a girl smells. Still, I decided that I wanted to clean up so I pushed Kip back into the wall while I copped a quick grab between his legs.

"There's a beer in the fridge. Grab one and give me a couple minutes. Hit the lights, too, would you," I said, tugging his dick a little, as I turned and went into the bathroom. I was going to be clean, for sure, but did not need him asking about the scars that threaded the insides of my thighs.

I came out of the shower, turned off the bedroom light. I opened the door and leaned against the frame. I had nothing on. Nothing. Not a stitch. I wanted to get right to it. No need to waste time with the usual bumbling, getting felt up over my shirt, the guy wondering whether he should reach under or not. Here I am. Let's get to it. Finish. Get him in. Get him out.

I stepped backward onto my bed. Kip walked right in, trying not to look too anxious. It was cute, and I was just as anxious, so I didn't mind. As he stepped close to the bed, I unzipped and pulled his jeans down, boxers too.

Crack, crack.

The next few minutes were a frenzied tangle of tongues and mouths, moans and sweat.

* * *

"Mind if I stay for a few?" Kip asked, when we were done.

I pulled the blanket up and clicked on the TV.

"Sure, but let's not make it a sleepover," I answered, trying not to be mean although, having no interest in any kind of relationship that had depth beyond my getting fingered, licked, and fucked, I really wanted him to go.

Kip sat up a bit and shoved a pillow behind his head. He looked over at me, maybe a little sad, not that I cared.

"No problem," he said.

Maybe five minutes or so into a particularly frantic episode of *Deadliest Catch*, Kip started reaching around under the covers.

He made a weird face, curling his lip up a bit.

"Shit," he said.

"Shit what?" I asked.

"My gum. I think I lost it in your bed somewhere," he said.

Thinking about it, I had not heard any cracking for some time. I guess I just assumed he threw it out. Maybe swallowed it.

"Maybe you put it in the trash," I said, just as he burrowed his head under the covers.

"No I didn't," was the muffled reply as I felt his hand on my crotch.

I jumped a bit. "Hey, come on, I'm done for the night," I said.

He pulled his head out from under the covers.

"I know and, shit, I'm sorry, but, I think you're going to want to get up," he said, looking like a little boy who just ate the last Oreo.

Something about him at that moment caught me as funny and I wanted to laugh, but I controlled the urge, doing my best to appear irritated instead.

"What's the problem?" I asked.

He was on his elbows, head in his palms. "I found the gum," he said.

"Okay, so get it and toss it on your way out." Now I was getting annoyed.

"Well, you better do it," he said, pulling my hand down.

The gum was stuck in my pubic hair, the little of it I had.

"Well, thanks for that," I said, starting to laugh.

"Anytime," Kip said, laughing back as he pulled his jeans on.

THIRTY-ONE

JB

I remembered how there was nothing easy about taking four young kids to the beach. Loaded coolers, blankets, towels, and diaper bags. Shovels and bags of sand toys over one shoulder, umbrellas strapped to the other. A backpack full of sunscreens stuck to my skin as I sweated and trudged, like an old burro, over the hundred or so feet of searing sand to just the right spot where we would set up our small township for the day. Once we were settled, the family version of "boots on the ground," chairs and blankets firmly planted, family days at the beach were generally a replay of the day before. Hours were spent building castles that didn't get finished or were stomped on by some kid blindly chasing a sand crab. We doled out juice boxes, bags of chips and PB&Js like vending machines. The eating blended seamlessly into the cleanup, usually with Laurie or me running after a plastic wrapper or paper plate as it blew down the beach, always just out of reach. The girls liked the water, but when they were little, could only go to the edge and, even then, Laurie made them wear those inflatable swimmies on their arms, which they uniformly hated. Not that I could blame them. It was hot and their little arms were engulfed in plastic filled with as much air as I could manage to blow in. We would stand at the water's edge and, one at a time, the girls would stand in front of me extending their arms out so that I could grab their hands and yank them up into the air, just as the water crested over their toes. A lot of times, while I was there in body, but in spirit, I was somewhere else. On a lazy horizon of sand, with waves rolling in and out, and definitely with a cold beer in my hand. Where no one cried or needed food or had a sandy diaper waiting to be changed.

Now, by myself on Juno Beach, I thought about those times.

It was a picture book afternoon. Marshmallow clouds danced

across a chalkboard of baby blue. I pinched some sand between my toes and sipped from a can of Bud, squeezed inside a red-and-white Coca-Cola koozie that I bought at the convenience store on the way to the beach. Looking at the beer, I shook my head, thinking of my little girls' arms jammed into those inflatables all those years ago. I thought about the scene in Thornton Wilder's play *Our Town* when Emily asks, "Does anyone ever realize life while they live it...every, every minute?" and the actor playing the stage manager answers, "No. Saints and poets maybe...they do some."

I sure didn't realize life back then, while I was living it. And now, I thought, here I am, alone.

* * *

Having finished one of the two cans of Bud I brought for the afternoon, I yanked the other out of a disposable Styrofoam cooler that was already falling apart from an hour or two of use. Right about the time I was jamming Bud number two into the koozie and getting ready to sing along with Southside Johnny on a few songs from his *Better Days* live album, I heard a woman's voice, screaming from the ocean.

Predictably irritated, I pulled myself out of the chair, took a long swig from the beer and looked out into the water. Without my contacts on, everything beyond the end of my arm was pretty blurry, but I could make out someone in white, not too far out, bobbing up and down, flailing her arms around. She was the screamer. I grabbed an old pair of glasses from my bag to see better and could tell that there was definitely a woman out there, waving, and no, it didn't look good. Farther out and off to the left a bit, I could make out what looked like two people floating, maybe on a boogie board or raft. I took a quick look around the beach. Other than a whale of an older dude asleep on his back, whose distended belly was thrust toward the sun, it was only me.

I watched the fellow's belly rise and fall, rise and fall. One of those jelly roll things from Spencer Gifts, I thought. The guy was covered only by a royal blue Speedo and sunscreen that was not completely rubbed in over a mound of chest hair that blew to the left with the ocean breeze.

As the woman continued to scream, I glanced down the beach and pondered my next move. I thought about waking the fat guy, but when I looked closer, it was clear that he must have been having quite the dream, as he was rod hard, his Speedo stretched in a way that no one in public really needed to see. I'd like to think it was bravery, but in reality I decided that going in after the drowning lady was infinitely preferable to waking the sleeping giant with a boner.

As soon as I got in the water, I was swimming faster than I ever had before, zipping through the waves like Aquaman. Adrenaline, I thought at first. Once I got out to where I figured the lady would be, however, I realized that adrenaline had nothing to do with it. I was in deep water and was definitely in the middle of a riptide. One of those things that leads to news stories that always include a mention of a body being washed on the shore six miles away. Anyway, I treaded some and looked around, but could not see the screaming lady. And, of course, the only thing I could hear was the sound of the ocean bellowing, with me feeling more and more like its late afternoon prey.

After a few minutes, I guess, I noticed a white strand in the water. As I swam closer, I could see that the white strand was a string from a bikini, and the white bottom was there as well. The screaming lady was now face down, black hair spread across a flushed whitecap, as if out of a horror movie. I grabbed the bikini top and pulled, just as another wave washed over. The woman's head bobbed up, across my chest, eyes rolled into the back of her head, and then flopped back into the water. Dead, I was sure, but I pulled again, this time with my left arm and as she popped back up, her pupils returned to their rightful state just as her top came off. Nice tits, actually, I remember thinking, just as she puked all over me.

Before I could react to being covered in a mix of vomit and salty seawater, the woman became frantic and started trying to climb on to my shoulders, pressing me down into the water over and over again. Each time I was able to free myself from her groping arms and out from under the soles of her feet just in time to grab a breath of air, another wave spanked me, shoving me right back under the tide. To make matters worse, she started the screaming again.

"We're going to die! My boys. We're all going to die," she yelped, continuing to maintain a half nelson around my throat, while coughing and gagging, over and over again. By about the third chorus predicting our demise, I had it figured out that the boys on the boogie board, floating out to sea, were her two sons.

I don't know how long this went on, but at some point, I was able to get her off my back and cradle her under my left arm while trying to paddle down shore with my right. I remembered from watching some show on the Discovery Channel that a riptide is not very wide and that you needed to avoid the urge to fight the current and instead swim parallel to the beach, through the tide and then, when it subsides, back toward shore. Knowing what I was supposed to do, however, had little impact on what I could actually do, while simultaneously trying to tow a deranged topless woman to safety.

A few minutes passed, or ten or fifteen maybe, but whatever it was, I just got tired. I couldn't fight her anymore and knew there was no way that I could keep swimming and pulling, swimming and pulling. I decided that the best course of action was to swim out with the tide and use it to take us out to the boys on the board. At least there, I could unload my cargo and she could be with her kids.

I got out to the boys without too much difficulty. Maybe eight and ten years old, they both seemed okay, despite the tears flowing down faces that were pale and afraid, so much so that I don't think either of them noticed their mother's naked breasts as she grabbed onto the board and squeezed in between the two of them. Once she was safe, I figured that someone must have seen us and would make a call to 911. In no time, the screaming mom and her boys would be back on the beach and no worse for the wear.

At that point, the smart thing for me, of course, was to hang on right there with them, one hand on a corner of the board, float and wait. But I didn't do the smart thing. Instead, I decided to leave the safety of the board and swim back in myself. I didn't get far before realizing, quite clearly, that I had chosen poorly. Whatever it was that got me through the last twenty or forty or however many minutes it had been, was gone. I was spent. I couldn't swim, I couldn't tread water, I couldn't move. My eyes, cloudy and misty from being soaked and pounded by the waves, were almost useless. I could hardly even make out the beach. I was breathing heavy, coughing up water; my throat was closing even as I tried to suck air into what must have been mostly fluid-filled lungs. I felt cold, yet clammy at the same time, like I did just before I would faint whenever I got a shot or got my finger pricked as a kid at the doctor's office. I had a resounding and persistent pounding between my temples.

I was drowning.

THIRTY-TWO

JB

What a way to go, I thought to myself. I was a hero, having just saved a woman who reminded me of Linda Blair from *The Exorcist*, head spinning around and retching green goo everywhere. Staying with my pre-death movie theme, I also thought of George Clooney at the end of *The Perfect Storm*, just as he recognized his fate and purposefully let himself go and drift underwater, peacefully sinking down and away into an ocean grave. Then I thought of my own grave, and what the headstone would look like. Jews don't put much on headstones, usually nothing more than "beloved" this or "cherished" that. Blinking feverishly, through the saltwater and my own tears, I think I saw mine, and it read something like *HERE LIES JOE BECKER. HE WAS PRETTY GOOD.*

I know it sounds silly, like some sort of feel good bullshit novel, but in that moment, I didn't want to just leave things having been "pretty good." I wanted something more, I really did, and now, as my heart pounded and exploded through my chest, I wasn't going to get it.

"Hey mister, you okay?" someone called.

I looked off to my right and saw the outline of a person, someone, I thought. I didn't really know, maybe this was the guy sent to ferret me off to heaven or wherever it was I was headed.

"I think so, yeah," is what I believe I said back to the guy.

"Take this," he said, tossing me some rubbery feeling thing on a rope. "Let's get you out of here."

THIRTY-THREE

JB

After an ambulance ride to the hospital that I didn't remember much of and a couple hours of being poked, stuck, and observed, I was released onto solid ground. When the nurse gave me the green light, I peeled the pink plastic bracelet off my wrist, grabbed a cab back to my hotel, and planned to do what any normal person would after a near drowning. Get drunk.

Although the water pressure in my room was a little low and the shower took longer than planned, I rubbed off the saltwater and antiseptic hospital scent bouquet with some hotel-issued Ivory soap. Barely toweling off, I tossed on some jeans and a T-shirt along with my newest pair of Frye boots in about two minutes. When I was a kid, I remember saving up for my first pair of Frye's. They were chocolate brown, had a bit of a heel, and a square toe. They looked good, but they took months to soften up and my feet hurt like hell for the first couple of weeks. Technology is an amazing thing, though. These new ones that I had bought before I left home were already soft and broken in. Even the soles looked like someone had been walking around in them for a good month or two before me.

I told the cabbie I wanted to head over to The Shipwreck in Jones Beach.

"That dump?" he said. It may have been a question, I'm not sure, but he knew where it was and dropped me off in front in less than ten minutes.

Other than a group of people with laminated lanyards on orange strings around their necks, enjoying an after work happy hour, there were maybe ten others in the place, all of whom were at the bar watching TV. Most of the heads were aimed at the two larger screens, both showing a replay of the 1996 Sugar Bowl between Florida and Florida State. Around to the right were a couple of empty stools, with a girl behind the bar, back to the customers and watching the local news on an older TV above her. I sat down at the bar stool that faced the girl's back. Her hair, I don't know what to call it. Years ago, in the seventies, it would have been an afro, but now it was something entirely different than what some guys had when I was in junior high school. The tight curls, copper and chestnut, circled around her head like soft, inviting halo. I had an irresistible urge to reach over and run my hands thru it.

"Oh, hi," the girl said, as she turned around.

Her tank top, more than a size too small, was pulled low, scooping down just over the outsides of her caramel-colored breasts. I quickly thought of the reach rule created by my friend, Baldwin, an old high school buddy. The reach rule was simple mathematics. The youngest woman that a guy can "reach for" is half his age plus seven. That meant, according to the rule that, at age 53, I could, in theory and as a single man, have sex with a woman who was no younger than 33. Setting aside my being married and all that, this girl was clearly not within Baldwin's chronological requirements and more than a little too young for me. That's okay, I thought. No harm in looking.

"Hi, again," she said. "You want to watch the game?"

"No, thanks. I seem to remember that Florida won that one."

"Really? I can't stand football. I just don't get it. I mean, other than the guys in those tight pants," she laughed. She was really pretty.

I smiled and said nothing, unable to come up with a witty response.

She kept talking. "I've had to watch that game like, I don't know, twenty, thirty times. And you're right, Florida wins, 52-20, by the way. People down here, they still think that coach—Steve Spurrier, I think is his name—is God or something. I just think he looks stupid, wearing those awful blue and orange colors. Not to mention the dopey visor. Why not just wear a hat?"

I wasn't sure if she was really asking me the question or it was just normal bar chat, but she had a point. I never did get the whole visor thing. They do look dumb, now that I thought about it.

"Anyway, baby, what can I get you?" she asked, leaning forward with her elbows on the bar.

She called me "baby." She had long eyelashes. With every blink, I felt myself edging closer to when I was a sixteen-year-old boy, getting uncontrollably harder, like when I was in the cafeteria in tenth grade and the thing kept popping up while I was eating my Fritos. I almost forgot that I would have had to be probably eighteen years younger for her to be in the reach zone — and for me to be in hers.

It struck me right about then that I might pass for a playground stalker without the furry moustache. I looked away from the girl and leaned into the bar, pulling the stool closer and tucking my legs all the way under. I asked her for a Bud.

I pretended to watch the news when the girl pulled the bottle opener from inside the back of her shorts to crack open my long neck. A news reporter was on the beach and, although I could not hear much over Glen Frey and the rest of the Eagles singing "Take It Easy," the headline on top of the screen read, "Mom and Kids Almost Drown," while closed-captioning ran below.

"An Indiana mother and her two children on vacation were pulled from the Juno Beach surf today by an off-duty lifeguard. Although the lifeguard, Quinn Canter, brought all three in on a boogie board from almost a half mile offshore, the real hero was an unidentified man who swam in from the beach and saved the mom, Melanie Tate, from drowning. The gentleman took Melanie to her two young boys, who had inadvertently drifted out beyond the rip current and were unable to get back to shore. After saving Melanie, our hero almost drowned trying to get back to the beach, but was assisted by the lifeguard and taken to a local hospital. We don't know his name, but whoever you are, if you're watching, we have a message for you."

The camera panned to my lady in the white bikini, now with her top on. "Thank you," she said, blowing a kiss and exaggerating a smile at the camera. Taking a big swig from my beer, it seemed practiced and insincere, like the football player who says, "I'm going to Disneyworld," after winning the MVP at the Super Bowl. Give me a break. You want me to believe that this quarterback, six four and chiseled top to bottom, with millions of dollars and roughly the same amount of women in tow, is going to Disneyworld? Get the fuck out of here.

I felt nauseated.

"Happens all the time around here. Idiots drown in those riptides seems like every week," the girl said from behind the bar, snapping the channel over to the old Sugar Bowl game.

I felt like saying, "Hey, that was me. I'm the hero," but I didn't. And I wasn't. I was one of the idiots. I just happened to be a lucky one.

"I'm Macy, by the way," the girl said, leaning well across the bar top. Up close.

"I've never seen you around here," she said.

I wrapped my hand around the long neck of the Bud. "My first time here. I am looking for a friend. Actually, my friend's daughter. My dead friend's daughter." I was blathering.

"Shit," Macy said. "I know who you are. You're Uncle Bro, right? Sorry about that," suddenly uncomfortable and pulling her hand and her top back across the bar.

Absolutely nothing to be sorry about, I thought to myself.

"Hey, Jess," Macy hollered, as she turned and walked around the backside. I was still thinking of Macy when I felt a pair of cold hands reach around my shoulders.

"Uncle Bro," Jess said, her arms squeezing me tight, like my own kids did when they were little. I put my beer down and put my hands onto hers. As I turned, I caught a glimpse of the inside of both her forearms.

Scars.

THIRTY-FOUR

Jess

I recognized him, even from behind, hunched over a beer. Uncle Bro was always easy to make out among my dad's group of friends. Most of them seemed more grown up; when they were over playing cards or visiting, many wore suits and ties, usually just having come from work. Not my Uncle Bro, he always wore jeans, boots, and a T-shirt. Although I noticed as a kid that he dressed differently than my father's friends, I think that, as I got older, his being a lawyer but not looking like one somehow made me like him more than the others. Now, he had a faded red shirt on over his jeans and the heels of his boots were hooked onto the wooden rung at the bottom of his barstool. I felt urgently reconnected again. Somehow, it was almost as if my father were there. I pressed my head into his and wrapped my arms around him without thinking about it.

"Thanks so much for coming. It's great to see you," I said, before he could turn around.

"Hey, Jess. You, too," he said, turning to meet me. "You look good. Different. Older," he said. I knew that he noticed my arms, which I couldn't really keep covered anymore in the sticky Florida heat.

"Well, I lost the makeup and the pink hair. Didn't really like it anyway, to be honest," I said.

"Neither did your mom, right?" he asked, knowing the answer.

I just smiled.

"Guess that's why you kept it, yes?" he asked, rubbing the top of my head. "Seriously, you do look great. It feels great to be down here. I don't think we've seen the sun back home for over a month," he said.

"I know, right? I haven't worn a coat in a year."

We got through the weather, and I didn't want to just jump into the talk about my dad or finding my biological family. I didn't really want to ask about my sister and didn't care about my mom. We both looked at each other, not exactly knowing what to say next.

"Nice place," he said, looking around the bar.

"Yeah, it's pretty cool. I like it here. I live with my friend, Macy, well next door actually. And Bobby, the manager, he also runs the apartment building I live in. A lot of the employees live there. It's just down the street. Called The Cove."

I was talking way too fast, hoping to avoid any more of those "what do I say next?" dilemmas.

"Hi, Uncle Bro. I'm Macy, your favorite bartender," Macy said, from behind the bar.

I appreciated her jumping in and breaking up my running commentary about life in Jones Beach.

"Yes, you are," said my Uncle Bro, looking at Macy in a way that I knew he meant it. I ignored it.

"Okay, so when do we start looking for my family? I mean my biological family," I asked him. I always hated it when people asked me if I knew my "real parents" since my mom and dad, Tom and Lianne, they were the only parents I ever had. The only parents I ever knew.

A lot of adopted kids have issues with knowing who they are, feeling different from the others in their family and that sort of thing. I felt those same feelings, I know, and while it's true that I had spent a lot of time since my move to Florida thinking about whether I was really meant to have grown up in some other place, somewhere else, I never once really thought my parents were somehow not my "real parents."

"That's why I am here, Jess. I have already started working on things for you. I want to fill you in," he said.

THIRTY-FIVE

JB

Jess plopped onto the barstool and leaned into me, pressing her palms into the stool and between her legs.

"Mace, can I have a shot of Jack?" She pointed to the bottle.

"Me too, Mace," I said.

"Here you go, Uncle Bro," Macy said, smiling and filling the short glass to the brim. As if I didn't feel old enough already, now I was "Uncle Bro" to another twenty-something girl that I couldn't take my eyes off of. For obvious reasons, Springsteen's "Girls in Their Summer Clothes" was spinning in my head—"the girls in their summer clothes pass me by." I sighed and wrapped my hand around the shot glass.

I have been in a lot of bars over the years. Many where they have those metered bottle spouts, giving you a perfect, impersonal and disappointingly insufficient amount of whiskey. Not here. "Nice pour," I thought to myself.

Jess shot hers back without a pause. It clearly wasn't her first. I followed suit, and looked over at Macy. She refilled the glass as I began giving Jess the rundown.

"Keep in mind that adoption, in the old days, was meant to be kept secret. And when I say 'old days,' I mean as recent as 1992, at least in Maryland," I said.

But I was born in Pennsylvania, right?" she asked.

"Good question. Yes. You were, but the adoption itself, the legal piece of it, that was in Maryland."

"Okay," she said. "Sorry."

"No, ask away. Really. It's good that you want to understand everything. Anyway, in Maryland, adoptions filed up until 1992 are sealed and cannot be accessed by the public. So, what I am saying is that we could not just go across the street and get the file from the courthouse, even though we knew you were formally adopted in Montgomery County. Remember those forms I had you sign?" I asked her.

She nodded.

"One was a power of attorney. It allowed me to act on your behalf in my communications with the Maryland Department of Human Resources, which maintains adoption records from throughout the state," I told her, maybe overdoing the lawyering details a bit.

She didn't seem to mind.

"Okay, go ahead," Jess said, scratching the inside of her right arm.

"From there, I was able to get what they call 'non-identifying' information about your adoption, most of which, to be honest, you probably already knew. You want all these details or just bottom line?" I asked.

"I want to hear it all, Uncle Bro, I have to," she said, still scratching.

I put my hand over hers, not saying anything, hoping she would stop. Watching her and that obsessive scratching at her arms, trying, it seemed to me, to pick or rub those scars away.

"Okay, so, acting on your behalf," repeating that stiff phrase, "I requested that we be put in contact with what they call a 'certified confidential intermediary.' Someone who has access to that non-identifying information and can then advise the Court as to whether it can be released to you."

"So, did that tell you who my parents were?" Jess asked.

"No, only some basics of the adoption, when you were born, where, again, stuff you already knew," I said. "However, since you are over 21, we were then able to ask the Court for your birth certificate," I said, as Jess cut me off.

"What good does that do? I have my birth certificate. It was issued in Maryland," she said.

"Yes, but your original was from Pennsylvania. Also, the law permits us to get all records that relate to the birth certificate. So,

I guess what I am saying is that I have a name. I know who your mom is. Your biological mom, I mean."

Her arms were now folded in front of her, hands tightly wrapped around her elbows. "But what about my bio dad?" she asked.

"Don't know. That box just says '*unknown*.' "Her name is Karen Standridge. Says she was twenty-two when you were born."

Jess didn't say anything. She didn't smile. She didn't cry. Nothing.

Maybe she didn't understand me, I thought.

"Your mom. That's your biological mom. Karen Standridge."

"I know what you meant," she said, as she stood up and walked away.

THIRTY-SIX

Jess

I had to get away for a minute. Just a minute is all. He did all that work. Came down here just to help me. Now all I could think of was how much I wanted him to leave. Get back on a plane. Go home, Uncle Bro. Leave me alone.

In my bar, pouring shots, showing my boobs, collecting tips. I am fine. I am. Was. Whatever.

My heart was beating in that way it does. Everything was sweaty. That gross, cold sweat. My hands. My face. My shirt was wet, soaked through and sticking to my back. Sitting on the floor just past the kitchen and outside the bathroom, I couldn't stop fidgeting. I started to grind my nails into the grout between the tiles. I couldn't breathe. I wanted to cry, so I tried, but the tears wouldn't come.

I couldn't really believe it. Karen Standridge? What did that even mean? Just a name. A woman's name. It meant nothing to me. Yet, somehow, it meant everything.

I don't know why I was feeling this way. It was so unreal to me, but why? I wanted to know, I did. I wanted to meet her. I needed to understand. Wasn't I good enough? Why did you send my sister and me away?

I knew what I needed. I looked around the kitchen. The guys were working, but either didn't notice me or just decided that I needed to be left alone.

A toothpick, a fork, the clip off a pen. Just something sharp. I could do it quick and no one would know. That would do it. Wash this wave away.

* * *

I stood up and grabbed a stray bottle opener from next to one of the refrigerators. I stuck it in my back pocket and turned toward the bathroom.

"No way, girl," Macy whispered, startling me a little from behind, wrapping her arms around my waist.

THIRTY-SEVEN

JB

I waited a few minutes, sipped what was left of my beer and did my best not to continue the old dude trying to flirt with a younger girl thing. That was made much easier when Macy slipped from behind the bar, having been replaced by a guy with a worn white apron and a mean case of teenage acne.

"What'll you have, my man?" he asked, rapping his knuckle on the bar. He reminded me of a convict who just got released after a few years in the state pen, all anxious and jittery, not knowing what to do or where to go first. I got this sense he wanted me to order something exotic just so he could try his hand at some snazzy mixology. I took a quick glance at the dude, confident that being behind the bar was not his usual spot.

"Bud's good, thanks," I answered, trying not to look directly at him.

Looking slighted, the fellow popped the top off the Bud and slid it across the bar to me, Western movie–style. I held my hand up and caught it, a hockey goalie making a save.

"Christ, Seeds, get your ass in the back," hissed another guy, about my age, maybe a little younger. Tall, long salt-and-pepper hair, the kind you see in Vidal Sassoon magazine ads. No beard, but not clean-shaven either. He was in jeans and a plain black T-shirt. Not one of those graphic tees you can buy at the mall. Just black.

"Sorry about that, man. He's great in the kitchen," the man said, stepping toward the temporary barkeep. "And that's where you need to be, Seeds. Tell Macy I need her out here. Not break time," he said, slapping Seeds on the shoulder, as if he were his big brother.

"Man," Seeds grumbled, ever so gently, as he walked through the swinging door and disappeared.

"Good guy, but needs to be where he needs to be," the guy said. "I'm Bobby. You must be Jess's uncle. Heard her mention you were coming down. Good to meet you," he said, looking directly at me, nodding and extending his hand across the bar.

I shook it and nodded back.

"Another?" he asked.

Having just started the beer that Seeds delivered to me not thirty seconds ago, I thought he was kidding.

"They go down fast around here," Bobby said. "The heat and all that."

"These go down fast in any weather," I said, taking a long swig.

"You're right about that. Anyway, let me find the girls. Get Jess back out here so you two can finish your talk," he said.

I wasn't sure what to make of the guy. He seemed nice enough. Definitely in charge of the place, but I got this sense that he was trying to be protective somehow. Sort of like me, when a boy came to pick up one of my daughters on a Friday night. Like that.

THIRTY-EIGHT

Jess

"You need to pull your shit together," Macy said, after wiping a few tears off my cheek. "This is nothing; after all you've been through, Jess. I mean it. Come on now; let's see what we do next. And I'm with you. No worries. We'll go find this Karen baby mama of yours and meet her together, if you want," she said.

I straightened up, blinked it away. The need to do it, to cut myself, it had passed. I held Macy's hand and squeezed. We walked back to the bar. I climbed on to the stool, next to Uncle Bro. Bobby was there, leaning over from behind the bar a few feet away. He was looking at me, a swizzle straw between his teeth. I didn't know what he was thinking, but liked that he was there.

"Okay, so now that we know who she is, how do we find her?" I asked Uncle Bro.

"Jess, I already went ahead and started on that for you," he said. "There's a lot of crooks out there calling themselves 'investigators,' looking to take advantage of girls, uh, people like you trying to find family members," he said.

"So, how do we know where to get help?" I asked.

"Ahead of you there, too," he said, looking at me, then across at Bobby, and back again. I had a quick sense that there was some strange vibe between the two of them.

"There are a couple of guys we work with back at the firm. Both are former Montgomery County cops and now they do some PI work for us. Decent, smart, best of all, honest. I called one, he asked around, and I got connected to this group called Kin Hunt. Sounds a little backwoods, I know, but my guy gave them a big thumbs-up," Uncle Bro said.

"So, do we call them and try to get them to help?" I asked.

"Jess, no worries. Did that too. I spoke with the owner, Kurt something, I can't remember his name," he said, pausing.

"Thanks, Uncle Bro. But I don't care about his name. Just want to know what we need to do to get them going," I said.

"No problem. Sorry. Anyway, he quoted me a fee. $2900 if he gets paid all at once, $3100 if over two months, and $3300 if over three," he said.

"But I don't have that kind of money. Spent all I got from dad, plus my savings moving down here. Fuck."

He put his hand on my shoulder. "I paid it, Jess. Seriously, it's the least I could do. For you. For your dad," he said.

I thought I heard him say "for me, too" but I wasn't sure. He mumbled the last part.

"So, I paid him in advance, the $2900, figuring it would be a while before I heard back. Two days later, I got an email from Kurt telling me that my, I mean your, case was solved. That I should call him. So I did. Took him only two days, still can't believe it," he said.

"Okay, and then?" I asked. It felt like I was in the middle of a TV miniseries, the ones that stop each week right at the good part.

"I called Kurt. He filled me in, and then sent me an email. I thought you would rather see the note than hear it from me. Here you go," he said, handing me a wrinkled sheet of paper from his back pocket.

I looked at Uncle Bro and took that page. It felt weird. Here, in my hand, in this scrunched-up piece of paper was the connection to my history. Why I was given away. Who I am. How I got here.

"Don't worry, I can print another if you want to make some kind of scrapbook or something," he said.

I didn't say anything. I unfolded the paper and read it slowly, being sure not to miss a line.

Joe—here is the information we talked about. I went to the Pennsylvania State Birth Index and did a date and place search, knowing that the girl was born in Pittsburgh and you knew her birthday. As you can imagine, there were a lot of girls born in Pittsburgh on that day, but not too many sets of twins. I took a shot, figuring the girls were born at Magee, a busy women's hospital in Pittsburgh and sure enough there was only one set of twins born that day. Two girls. From there, I did a motor vehicles search on the name, and found her with no problem. Your client's biological mom is Karen Standridge. She lives in a place called Gallitzin, small town near Altoona. Was big into coal mining, now not exactly a ghost town, but close to it. 418 Church Street. So that's it. You can take it from here unless you want me to make the initial contact. I can go with her too if you want. Certainly wouldn't send the kid by herself. No extra charge. I do feel a little bit bad taking all the money since it took me like two hours to nail this down, but not that bad. Lawyer rates, right?

Thanks again,

Kurt

* * *

So, there it was. I handed the sheet to Macy. She put her arm around me. I looked over at Bobby, who was now leaning toward me from directly across the bar, his hand on top of mine.

"When can we go?" I asked.

THIRTY-NINE

Jess and Jamie

"Thanks so much for talking to me. I know it's been a long time, but I really needed to talk to you," I said.

"It so great to her from you, Jess. Almost a year, right? How have you been? How is Florida?"

It felt like I was catching up with an old friend, not my therapist. *"It's been good, really. I am doing pretty well down here. Working and paying my bills. It's all okay. I am, really. Okay. Remember my girlfriend, Macy? We live in the same building. Work together, too. I have made some other friends, so that's been good, too,"* I said.

With real friends, of course, it works both ways. I could have asked how she was doing, about the dogs, anything. But we weren't really friends. I just needed her help, that's all.

"So your email mentioned that you had some news and wanted to talk. I assume it's not about the nice weather down there. It's about forty-five and rainy here by the way. Haven't seen the sun in about a month, I don't think," she said.

"No, not the weather. Sorry about that. Sunny and eighty down here. The usual."

"Don't sound so disappointed. So, what's up?" she asked.

"I found my mom. My biological mom, I mean. My Uncle Bro, the lawyer, he helped me. She lives in some place with a weird name. In Pennsylvania," I said.

"That's great, Jess. Are you going to try to call her?" she asked.

"Gallitzin," I said.

"Bless you," she said.

"What?" I asked.

"It was a joke. Gallitzin. Sounded like you sneezed. Was joking. Sorry," she said.

I got it but didn't laugh. *"That's the town where she lives. My mom. My bio mom, I mean,"* I said.

"That's funny, Jess. I was in Gallitzin when I was a kid. There used to be a restaurant near there that my grandparents used to take me to. Ircolini's I think it was called. Ircolini's in Gallitzin. That's it. Amazing pies as I recall. Small world," she said.

"I don't think I'm going to call. Just going to go," I said. I wasn't too much interested in the pies.

"Let's talk about that, Jess," she said.

"Why not?" I asked. "Seems like the easiest way to me. Just go up, knock on the door, talk, and go from there."

"You don't think that would be kind of a shock to her?" she asked.

"Maybe. Sure. But why should I care? I've been wondering about her my whole life. How she decided we weren't good enough. Or maybe just me. I wasn't good enough. Kasey, well she is fine. Probably did not want to split twins up so I dragged Kasey with me." I forced a laugh.

"Whatever her reasons for letting you girls go, for putting you up for adoption, they were her reasons. I think just showing up on her doorstep unannounced, twenty-three years later, it might be difficult for her."

"For her? What about me? I asked.

"You're the one who is going. Call her, give her a few days anyway, and then plan the visit. A little time to let it settle in. What do you think?" she asked.

I did trust Jamie. What she said usually made sense. Here, though, I just wanted to barge in. Ask the lady? Why? Karen Standridge, what was wrong with me?

"Okay, I'll call first," I said.

"Good," she said. "Now, tell me what you're expecting from the visit."

"What do you mean by that? I'm expecting to ask her questions, have her answer them. She will wrap her arms around me; tell me it was the biggest mistake of her life, giving me up, that she wants me to come to little Gallitzen and live, do whatever they do there. Bake pies," I said.

"Still leaning on sarcasm to get you through, I see. A year and a thousand miles hasn't changed that, huh?" she asked.

"Guess not."

"Seriously, Jess. What if she doesn't want to talk to you? Have you thought about that?"

"No," I answered.

"I think you need to prepare yourself for that possibility, Jess. She may not be able to handle you coming into her life. You need to be ready for that. The rejection you might feel," she said.

"I—I hadn't thought about it. I just want to meet her. That's all I have thought about," I said. "More so, since my Dad died."

"Of course, she might also be really happy. She might have as many questions for you as you do for her. I just want you to be ready for the many possibilities is all," she said.

"I get it, I think. Thanks," I said.

"Remember, she could be very different from you. Gallitzin is a long way from Montgomery County. Very different," she said.

"Yeah. Okay." I wasn't sure what to say. Up to now, I just figured Karen would be falling down happy to see me. The idea that it would be anything else had not really crossed my mind.

"You're not going by yourself, are you, Jess?" Jamie asked.

"No, I'm good there. Macy and Uncle Bro are coming with me. Then I have to come to Maryland. My dad's unveiling thing," I said.

"Okay, good. How about you swing by and see me before you head back to sunny Florida?" she asked. "Just a quick check-in. Let me know how it went. I'd love to see you," she said.

You want to be sure I don't start carving little lines across my arms and legs, I thought.

"Maybe, sure. If there's time," I said before hanging up.

FORTY

JB

It felt good to be helping someone. Rarely in my business does anyone appreciate the work I do, much less take the time to thank me for it. I used to think that getting the bill paid was thanks enough, and to be fair, it should be. Do painters get thanked? Coal miners? Don't think so, no. I am not sure why I somehow think being a lawyer should be any different. I learned a trade, I do my job and I am supposed to get paid for it. That's it. Stop bitching and shut up.

This thing with Jess, though, it felt different. I really was doing something good. Something right. Meaningful. Not just for her, although that would have been enough. It was more than that. This was as much for me, as much for Tom too, as it was for Jess.

* * *

It was good to have Tom here with me; back on the beach in the same spot I was a couple of days ago. I almost died here, I thought.

The waves splashed and dogs barked. The sun beamed down on me. Not too hot. Warm. Perfect.

He was in the chair next to me, smiling in that way he did. At nothing. At everything.

"Nice, huh?" he asked.

"Yeah. Been a long time since I felt this good. Relaxed, you know?"

"I know. Pass me a beer," Tom said, leaning forward and peering over his sunglasses, his California blonde hair tasseled and blowing in the wind.

I twisted off the top and handed him a cold Rolling Rock.

Tom laughed. "How about that. Nothing like an ice cold Rock, right Bro?" he said.

I cracked mine open, took a drink. "Got that right, Tommy boy," I answered.

Girls walked by. Long, tanned legs. Small bikinis. They turned and smiled at us, each and every one.

"Yeah, baby," Tom said.

We clanked our long necks together and drank again.

Elton John was "crocodile rocking" on the radio.

I pinched sand through my toes, feeling the scratch of each grain.

"You're doing the right thing, man," Tom said, leaning up out of his beach chair.

I nodded.

"Least I can do, buddy. You'd do the same," I said.

"I know. Still, thanks, man. Really. Thanks," he said.

"You're welcome," I said.

I opened my eyes.

FORTY-ONE

Jess

I knew we only had a few days before heading up to Pennsylvania, but after talking to Jamie, I had a hard time thinking about what I should say. Somehow it seemed easier just to go there with no phone call first. Like yanking off a Band-Aid, it might hurt, but then it's over and done.

It's crazy the things you can find on the Internet these days. All it took was a quick Google search and I got ahold of a recommended script for adoptees when they call their birth parents. I printed the script, filled in the blanks, and made the call.

"Hello." A woman's voice.

"Hi. My name is Jess Porter. I was born at Magee Women's Hospital in Pittsburgh, Pennsylvania, on July 7, 1982. I was a twin. Did you give up twins for adoption?" I asked, following the script exactly.

I held my breath.

There was a short silence. Then a voice.

"Hi, Jess. Yes. That was me. I have been waiting for this call. I never changed my name, even after I got married. Always made sure my number was listed, just in case you or your sister tried to call me," she said.

Suddenly, I flared. That pissed me off. Out went the script. "That's great. Thanks. Why didn't you try to call us?" I asked.

She explained something about not having money, not knowing how to start. My head was buzzing, so I didn't catch it all.

"Are you married? Any children?" she asked.

"No and no. I'm only twenty-three." Those seemed like dumb questions to me.

"Oh. Sorry. Just thought I would ask," she said.

I remembered what Jamie told me. About her being different.

"That's okay," I said. I was hoping that I could come up for a visit in a couple of days. I know it sounds quick, but—"

Before I could finish, she cut me off.

"Sure. I can't wait," she answered.

"I'll have some friends with me, if that's okay," I said.

"Of course," she said.

I wasn't sure, but it sounded like she was crying.

"Okay, great. See you Thursday," I said, crying too.

FORTY-TWO

Jess

"You've been here about a year, Jess," Bobby said. "It's no problem. Taking some time off." He was sitting at the end of the bar looking over last night's receipts. Same thing every day.

"Cookin' the books, boss?" Cary asked, craning his head through the service window, leather hat in place.

"Yep. Trying to figure out some way to keep you on the payroll, dipshit," Bobby answered, his head still down.

I was behind the bar, towel drying the GET WRECKED OR GET OUT shot glasses, standing between the two of them. I smiled at Cary who was looking through the window at Bobby. He started to laugh, but thought better of it. Bobby wasn't serious. Or maybe he was. Cary ducked back into the kitchen, not wanting to find out.

With the sound of dishes being stacked, Bobby returned to me. "With both of you out, though, it's going to get a little tight," he said, head still angled down into the paperwork and his laptop.

"I know, sorry. I think she figured I needed someone with me," I said. "I could just tell her no, that I'm okay, if you want." I wasn't sure what he wanted.

He looked up and at me, stroking his hair, streaked with some gray, from front to back. Those eyes, black sometimes, but blue at others, beamed on me.

"But you're not okay," Bobby said. "It's better if Macy goes with you. That way, I know you'll be back from 'wherever the hell it is,' Pennsylvania," he said.

I kept rubbing the glass, looking back at him. Was this a big brother kind of thing? Did he care about me that way? Maybe, he liked me. I could be his girlfriend. Maybe he loved me even.

I kept at the drying, wondering. Not likely, I thought.

Probably just wanted to make sure his wait staff was not taking off for good.

It wasn't just Cary. He was hard to read.

The glass squeaked, obviously dry.

"I think you're good," Bobby said.

* * *

"What? Yeah, I am fine," I said.

"I meant the glass," he said, nodding.

"Oh. Yeah. Sorry," I said, putting it under the bar and grabbing another.

"And what's with that JB, Uncle Bro guy?" he asked. "Looks awful interested in you. Macy too, to be honest."

"He was my dad's friend. Practically grew up over at his house. My dad took me over there whenever something bad happened at home and my mom was going to kill me," I said. "He seems kind of sad, don't you think?" I asked.

"I don't know about that, but sure, if you say so." Bobby covered my hand with his. "Just come on back," he said.

"Ain't that some kind of sex harassment?" Cary was back, pleased with himself.

Bobby pulled his hand away, his head back into his work. Profits. Losses.

I didn't move. The hairs on my arm, just above where his hand had been, even if it was for just a few seconds, were still standing.

FORTY-THREE

Jess

"How about we try this restaurant my therapist told me about?" I asked, from the backseat.

After the flight from West Palm Beach up to Baltimore and a short shuttle ride to Uncle Bro's car at the Quick Park lot, we hopped onto the highway and headed toward Gallitzin. I didn't much feel like talking so I sat in the back, leaving Macy to sit up front with Uncle Bro.

"Don't you want to get there and see her?" Macy asked.

Uncle Bro didn't say anything, but he glanced back at me through the rearview mirror.

Once we got onto the road, I really did not know how I was going to sit for another three hours. I told myself that I could sleep and then before I knew it I would be up and we would be there.

* * *

Of course, I couldn't sleep. I never could sit still for too long anyway. As a kid, any car rides longer than maybe twenty minutes were a nightmare for me. I needed something to keep me busy. Crayons, markers, some sort of toy to pull, tug at, and more than a few times, toss at my sister's head. It wasn't much better as an adult except that if I was the driver, it didn't seem to bother me. For this ride, though, it wasn't just my usual hyperactivity. The bit about meeting my mother for the first time, that didn't help either.

"No, seriously, let's get something to eat first," I said to Macy. Can you find out where that Ircolini's place is?"

I knew we were getting close. Some time ago we had passed signs for Route 70, Pittsburgh, and Harrisburg. The ones for Edensburg and Hollidaysburg, too.

"Shit, lots of 'burgs' up here in Pennsylvania, huh, JB?" Macy asked. I wasn't sure when she shifted from calling him Uncle Bro to JB.

"Yeah, but we are getting close. Once we get through Altoona, we'll be about there," he said.

"No Ircolini's," Macy said. "I googled it. Says they closed a long time ago," she said. "Anyway, you need to put your big girls on and le'ts get over there," Macy said, turning to reach over the seat and squeeze my knee.

"It's okay," Uncle Bro said. "Let's go to the Horseshoe Curve."

"The what curve? And why? She needs to get this done, meet this lady," Macy said.

"The Horseshoe Curve. It's famous. Historic place. And I think they have a diner or something there. We can grab something to eat. Jess can collect herself. It's fine," he said.

Uncle Bro looked back up at me again. A quick wink kind of thing and smiled.

I almost said it out loud, but stopped in time.

It wasn't him, but I thought it anyway.

Thanks, Dad.

FORTY-FOUR

JB

I could tell she wasn't ready. We were all hungry and a little cranky after the several hours of travel. Even though I knew Jess's mother would be waiting for us, there was no harm in stopping for a while. Probably a good thing, actually. Get some fresh air, walk a bit after all the travel. Plus, being the history nerd I am, even something offbeat like a quirky railroad track, got me going. I really did want to see the thing.

"Let's take a quick look in the museum," I said, after parking the car. I know the girls heard me, because they were following, but I was too excited to notice if either said anything.

We walked up the path past several trains and boxcars, into the redbrick Railroaders Memorial Museum. "Very cool, right?" I asked. I looked back at Jess and Macy.

As if on cue, they both nodded and smiled.

"Yeah, Uncle Bro, this looks great," Jess said.

"Love me some rusty old trains," Macy said.

Both looked at me as if it wasn't going to be long before I needed help eating my oatmeal.

"Opened in 1854. Built by hand, no machines. Almost entirely by workers from Ireland," I said, reading from the brochure.

"Love me some Irish," Jess said. She and Macy broke out laughing.

"They worked twelve-hour days. Twenty-five cents an hour. Bent over, digging, banging in railroad ties. Different world," I said.

"Bet they didn't have to bend over and show their titties all day to a bunch of drunk college kids," Macy said.

"Yeah, that's real work," Jess added.

"Very funny, you two," I said.

"And look at this. The Nazis tried to have the place blown up

136

during World War II," I said. "I didn't know that."

"Wish they had," Macy said.

"Seriously, Uncle Bro, can we eat and get going?" Jess said.

"The tour only takes 45 minutes. It'll be fun," I said, trying to herd the girls into the small line that was forming at the far wall.

"Pass," said Macy, turning and heading toward the door.

"Maybe next time, okay Uncle Bro?" Jess said, trailing Macy and still holding her hand.

I folded the brochure down the middle and jammed it in my back pocket.

FORTY-FIVE

Jess

We all got the same thing for lunch. A sandwich, Lay's chips, and a soda in a paper lunch box made into the shape of a train. Macy and I both laughed when we got to the table, but I was so hungry it didn't matter that the sandwich may have been as old as the Horseshoe Curve. We didn't talk much and I thought that Uncle Bro was annoyed that we wouldn't stay and take the tour or look in the museum for a while.

After we ate, Macy and I went to pee and clean up. Looking in the mirror, I was washed out, mostly from not sleeping and traveling all day.

"Jesus Christ, Jess. You can't meet your mama looking like that. Stay here, I'll go grab some stuff from the car," she said.

I didn't want to look like some sort of weirdo hanging out in the bathroom, so I ducked into a stall and waited the couple of minutes until Macy got back. Was I wearing the right clothes? I didn't know. I had on some jeans, a gray pullover long-sleeve cotton T-shirt and a new pair of Chuck Taylors that I needed to break in before wearing them to work. Nothing that would make me stick out. No chance that anyone could see the scars on my arms.

"Jess, where are you girl?" I heard Macy as she got back into the bathroom.

I stepped out of the stall.

"You can't go looking like some run-down, beat-up white girl," Macy said.

"I am a run-down, beat-up white girl," I said, trying to make a joke.

"Okay, Jess. Pull yourself up and let's get to it. You've been through a lot. You are making your own way in this world. It's something to be proud of. Head up, girl," she said, pressing her palm under my chin.

I looked up; my hands limp at their sides.

Macy propped herself up on the sink facing me. She applied some eyeliner and a slight bit of lipstick.

She reached my arms and pulled them up, as if I were a toddler whose mom was helping her get dressed.

A couple of women came in and out of the bathroom and were probably confused watching Macy dress me, but other than a few looks, no one said anything.

"Let's get rid of the old gray T-shirt," she said, handing me a light blue V-neck sweater.

She pulled off my T-shirt, exposing a lacy black bra underneath.

"Nice," Macy said. "But let's keep those covered until you meet yourself a rich Gallitzin guy."

We couldn't stop laughing. She fixed my hair. I felt better.

Pretty.

Ready.

"I love you, Mace," I said.

"You too, Jessie girl," she said.

FORTY-SIX

Jess

We turned into the gravel driveway just past a black metal mailbox with stick-on numbers that told me it was 418 Church Street. A chain-link fence ran along the gravel on the right, enclosing a grassy front yard. A couple of skinny shepherd-looking dogs barked and jogged alongside the car from across the fence. The driveway wasn't that long, really. It just seemed that way to me. I watched the dogs, listened to the sound of them barking, the car tires crackling a symphony of percussion on the rocks below. It was like I was in a slow-motion home video.

There was a nice front porch. The house somehow seemed a lot more sophisticated than I thought it would be. It was a pretty little yard with a big tree, an old tree, right in front. No weeds. Some flowers where they should be. I half expected her to live in a trailer, wearing someone else's old Crocs or some such thing. But this place was fine, attractive even.

I got out of the car.

* * *

There were a few people on that porch. Five or six maybe. All were smoking and drinking. Some beer I couldn't recognize from where I was outside the car. I really tried, but couldn't figure it out. The cans did not look familiar to me. Of all the things to be worried about, here I was trying to guess the brand of beer my bio mother drank.

"Jess," Uncle Bro said, patting me on the back. "It will all be fine."

"Yeah, but what beer is that?" I thought to myself. I knew that Rolling Rock was a Pennsylvania beer. Used to be, anyway.

"Jess, I think that's her," he said.

I snapped out of my beer detective mode as a woman came down the steps of the porch.

It was a big lady. Really big. Not a little fat, mind you. Oh no. One of those "three trips to the all you can eat buffet" types. Not at all pretty. A meatball with boobs.

My brain went into overload. I hoped that wasn't her, I thought. Oh, fuck, I'm screwed. I'm destined to be a moose, chowing on Big Macs. Everything supersized. All my clothes would be from Ross, that awful store for blubbery chunkers.

I was sweating.

Like a pig.

FORTY-SEVEN

Jess

"Hi, I'm Karen." She hugged me tight.

Looking at the other people on the porch, my head squished into her shoulder, I was thinking how glad I was that she didn't try to kiss me.

She smelled like one of those drugstore perfumes my mom bought Kasey and me when we were little.

"It's so good to meet you, Jessica," she said.

It did feel good. The hug. Something I can't remember getting from my mom. Lianne. But didn't she, Karen hug me like this before? When I was a baby? Sure she did. She hugged me. Then she gave me away.

I pulled back. "It's Jess. Just Jess," I said.

"Oh, I . . . well, I just thought, well, sorry," she said.

"Shit, she's been called a lot of things. Worse than that, trust me. No worries." Macy to the rescue.

"Haven't we all?" Karen said, smiling at me, relieved.

"I'm Macy," she said. "And I'll take a hug, too."

Karen hugged her.

"And, Tom, it's been such a long time. You look good. Your hair looks darker than I remember," Karen said. "Thanks to you and Lianne for taking care of my baby. She is beautiful. I'm so grateful."

She wrapped her arms around Uncle Bro. Big hugger, this lady.

Uncle Bro looked at me. He didn't say anything. Waiting for me, I guessed.

"He's not Tom. He's not my dad," I said. "My dad's dead."

Karen pulled back from him, turning toward me. I thought she might cry.

In just a couple of minutes, I had already made this lady feel bad once. It didn't seem right for me to do it again.

* * *

"It's okay, Karen. He's my dad's best friend. My Uncle Bro. A stand-in, I guess you could say," I said.

"That's right. Been a stand-in my whole life," Uncle Bro said.

"What kind of beer you got?" Macy asked.

FORTY-EIGHT

Jess

I waited a few seconds, filing behind Macy and Uncle Bro on my way up the stairs to the porch. Karen was up on the porch, hugging another heavyset woman.

"This is my sister, Ann. Your aunt," she said.

Ann was another heifer. That was all I could think about as I extended my hand to shake hers.

But when I looked again, Ann was actually pretty in a middle-school teacher kind of way. Light brown hair cut in a bob style and soft brown eyes. She did have a big, round face, but had on some pretty makeup and unlike Karen, did look like she tried to put herself together. I liked her hair, but thought to myself that someone with such a big face, well, she should let her hair grow some.

"That's not going to work around here, baby," she said, setting her beer on the top of the rail and wrapping her arms around me.

Waiting for what I thought was a fair amount of time, I pulled away from Ann and asked her for a beer.

"She wants an Iron City, Kay," Ann said to Karen.

Kay? Must be her nickname, I thought.

"Can't take the Pittsburgh out of the girl," Ann said.

Okay, sure, I thought. *I've never even been in Pennsylvania, much less Pittsburgh.* I took the beer and had a swig. I liked it.

"So, Kay, introduce your baby to everyone here," Ann said.

"Oh, sorry, I'm just so excited," Karen said, beer in one hand, cigarette in another.

Using her hand with the cigarette, she put her arm around the back of the guy standing next to her. He was in jeans and what I could tell was a new shirt. It was checkered in red and blue and still had the folds from the packaging across the chest. Not surprisingly, it was tight around his belly, one button just waiting to blow.

"This is my boyfriend, Jerry," she said.

"Hey, Jess, good to meet you," he coughed, beer still in his mouth. Just the fact that I could understand what he said with a mouth full of Iron City was impressive.

She went around the rest of the porch, introducing me to the others.

There was Janet, assistant manager downtown at the "five and dime," whatever that was. Tammy, a bottle blonde, showed me her ring. She got married a few weeks ago, but her husband is a truck driver and he was out on a run, so she came by herself. "Little Tim," who was anything but, came by from next door. He and Karen had lived next door to each other for more than ten years. There were a few others, but with all of them cranking on the Marlboros and Iron City, it was hard to remember who was who.

"What about my father?" I asked.

Ann and Karen started to talk at the same time. Karen waved her off. "It's okay," she said.

"Your dad, he's dead. He's dead too," she said.

FORTY-NINE

JB

"Oh, Christ," I said, a little too loud.

I wasn't sure how much more this kid could take. First her dad, her real dad, my friend, Tom, up and dies on her. She bounces between drugs and alcohol and prescription meds. She cuts herself; she even I think tried to kill herself a few years back. Now finally, she's getting somewhere and decides to do something brave. She traipses more than a thousand miles to find some answers and gets this. Another dead father.

Up to that point, I thought things were going well. Jess seemed interested in Karen and her sister, learning about her biological mom and where she grew up. Karen told her about dropping out of school, how she and her husband, Jess's biological dad, met at what she called a "woods party."

"What is a 'woods party?" I asked, sensing I maybe could guess some of it, but was still curious.

"Really? You folks don't do woods parties down in Maryland?" Karen asked.

"I mean, yes, we have woods, and of course, we have parties, but it's not like we all got together in high school and said, 'Let's have a woods party'," I said.

"Well, see, there's not much to do for kids around here. Back then, twenty or more years ago, even less," Karen said. There's two high schools nearby back then, Johnstown and Altoona. Hollidaysburg and Central Cambria, they came later. Anyway, on a Friday, someone would put the word out that we was having a woods party and spread it around to all the schools. Then a bunch of us would meet up, usually in this field down below the Curve, bring beer, joints, whatever. We would drink and smoke and all that bad shit you don't want your kids doing today," Karen said.

"You know about the Curve, the Horseshoe Curve?" Karen asked.

Before I could answer, Macy piped in. "We all know about it," she said.

"That's where Kay met your daddy, Jess," Ann said.

FIFTY

Jess

That pissed me off.

"Tom Porter was my father," I said.

"I know, right. I am sorry, Jess. You know, uh, I meant your, what do they call it, your natural daddy," she said.

"Biological, I think is what you mean," Uncle Bro said. Not mean or angry, but in a nice way. He raised his eyebrows at me, as if to say, *"Easy, girl, she didn't mean anything by it."*

"I understand, it's okay," I said. "Are there any pictures of him?"

I noticed Jerry, who was shaking his head as he turned the other direction, out toward the side of the yard.

"It's okay, baby. You know I love you," Karen said, kissing the back of his head. "Come on, Jess, I'll show you. Don't mind him. Jealous of a dead man. It is kind of sweet," she said.

She took my hand and walked me into the house.

Once inside, there was a small foyer, dark floors, and light blue walls. A pretty wood table next to the stairs. Fresh flowers in a glass vase.

"Lilies," she said. "Grow them out back."

"Over here I keep all my scraps. Scrapbooks, I mean," she said, walking into a small family room off to the right. We sat down on the couch.

"I could show you a bunch, but this is the best one. She opened a scrapbook, plastic covered and with cut-out magazine letters that spelled, *"Donny and Karen, New Orleans, 1991."*

Inside the book were pictures of the trip the two of them took before Kasey and I were born.

"I was pregnant with you and Kasey, but didn't even know it. Jesus, now I think about it. I was bad. We pretty much drank the whole time. I couldn't even count how many of those things I had, what do they call them, hurricanes? So good. Went down like water," she said.

Most of the pictures were from inside the French Quarter, drinks in their hands, walking on Bourbon Street. Donny, my father, looked sort of plain to me. A guy that would be hard to describe or pick out. Brown hair, brown eyes, not too tall, nothing that would catch your attention, I thought.

There was one, though, that did stick out. Donny had his shirt off, strands of beads around his neck, hands in the air, and drinks in both.

"Two fisting. Man loved that," Karen said.

His hair was long, pulled back, maybe even into a ponytail. I couldn't tell for sure. But with his hands up, one thing was for sure. Donny was one built dude. Lean, strong chest. Arms that popped and bulged. Muscles, you could see every one.

Karen sighed.

"Sorry," she said. "He was one piece of man, that is for sure."

"Yes, he was," I said, still looking at the photo and forgetting, just for a moment, that we were talking about my biological father.

FIFTY-ONE

Jess

"What's with the tattoos?" I asked.

The last page of the book was a picture of Karen and Donny. He was holding her leg across his chest with his right arm, flexing. It looked like his left arm was wrapped around Karen's back, probably to be sure she wouldn't fall. Both had the same tattoo, Donny's on his shoulder, Karen's on her ankle. A flower of some kind.

"It's a fleur-de-lis," she said. "You've seen it before. Ever watch football? It's on the New Orleans Saints helmets," she said, extending her leg out and turning so I could see it was still there.

"I like it, but why a football team? And aren't you guys all Steelers fans up here?" I asked. We had a big group of Pittsburgh people down at The Wreck who would come in on Sunday afternoons and watch Steelers games during the season.

"It's not really football. Means a lot more than that," she said. "In French, it's the 'flower of the lily' and stands for perfection, light, and life. We liked that, so we both got one when we were down in New Orleans," she said.

I hadn't asked, but assumed that Karen didn't go so far in school, and this was one thing she seemed to know a lot about.

"Also, like people's family crests and stuff, you can add different colors to add meanings. Like blue can mean truth and loyalty, red is strength, and green, my favorite, is hope, joy, and loyalty in love. I loved that so we had the tattoo guy design us this one in those three colors. Donny didn't want bright red on his arm, so that's why it's bordered in a faded out kind of red color. Still looks the same to me. You like it?"

"I do, yeah," I said. It was pretty and made me feel like I knew them, understood how much they meant to each other. How much in love they were.

"That was the best trip I ever took. Stayed in a fancy hotel and went to this one place where the bar turned around and around. Drinks were expensive there, so we just shared one. Donny set his on the bar while he was digging for some money and it started to move around the bar. Never seen him move so fast. He wasn't losing that drink, no way," she said, her eyes wet and blinking.

"I got one tattoo, a few years back. Really pissed my mom off," I said.

She asked to see it.

FIFTY-TWO

JB

"So what's it you do, JB?" Jerry asked, handing me a cold Iron City from the silver tub.

"Sit. They going to be in there awhile, most likely. You too, sorry, forgot your name, honey," he said.

"Name's Macy. Honey." Not one to be pushed around by anyone, that girl. She stared him down like a boxer at a weigh-in.

Ignoring or not noticing, either way Jerry was oblivious to Macy's pulse of anger. "And you guys are Jewish? Don't think I ever even met a Jew," he said.

"Jesus, Jerry, what the hell is wrong with you?" Ann asked.

"It's okay, no problem. Yes, Jewish. A lawyer, too," I said.

* * *

Although I grew up in an area with a fair number of Jewish people, there was still some anti-Semitism here and there. Once, in high school, I went to a card game with a buddy of mine to some guy's house who he knew from class. By the time we got there, the other guys had been playing and drinking for a while. I got tapped with the luck stick almost immediately, winning several hands in a row. After each hand, I was quiet, sweeping in the pile of dimes and quarters over to my side. Nothing like winning, sure, but when all was counted, at best I raked in eight bucks or so. Anyway, when we went to leave, one guy named Kettler or something like that made a crack along the lines of "there goes the Jew with all the money." I must have responded, although I can't remember what it was that I said. But it was enough to stand Kettler up from his chair and offer to meet me outside and "kick some Jew ass."

When describing my physique in those days, the only thing

that comes to mind is "scrawny." That said, I was not one to back down from a fight and immediately accepted the offer with a "let's go" nod as I walked toward the front door.

One of the many things I learned from my grandfather, a Navy vet, was that there was no such thing as an "unfair" fight. Before Kettler could get through the front door my fist, school ring and all, was waiting for him. Blood burst out of his nose and the fucker dropped like a stone.

* * *

With his well-earned beer gut and eyes that drooped like Goofy the Disney character, Jerry didn't look too tough. I figured, if need be, I could take him without too much trouble. "Seriously, no problem, Jerry. I'm not offended at all," I said. "So, how did you and Karen meet?"

"I was buddies with Donny. We knew each other from back in high school. Ran around, played some football, did everything together. Good guy," he said.

"I was due to be best man at their wedding," Jerry went on. "But then, shit, he went and died."

"Sorry. I understand," I said.

And I did.

"What happened?" I asked.

FIFTY-THREE

Jess

"That is one big-ass tattoo," Karen said, as I pulled my shirt back down, having shown her the butterfly on my back.

"I know. Too big, really. Felt right at the time, though."

"So, what's it mean. Why a butterfly?"

"Nothing. I just wanted something, and not a little girly heart or rose, either. No real reason. I knew my mom would be mad. Was wasted when I got it."

"I would have been mad, too," she said. "I mean, these things, they are forever, you know?"

"You can get them off," I said, a little smarmy maybe.

"Hurts, I hear," Karen said, ignoring the attitude.

"So, what happened? Donny, I mean," I asked.

"He was a good man, Jess. Worked hard and all that. Good to me. Just, well, not really right in the head, if you know what I mean?

"Not really, no," I said.

He had a lot of mental problems. Took medications. Was supposed to anyway. Doctors said he was bipolar," she said.

"Real moody, huh?" I asked.

"Yeah."

"Irritable a lot?"

"Mmmhmm."

"Lot of drugs and drinking I bet."

"That too."

"Trouble sleeping?"

"Every night."

"Wanted to fuck all the time?"

"Actually, I didn't mind that part. Sorry, too much there, huh?"

"That's okay," I said.

"How do you know so much about it?" she asked.

"I got it, too," I said, pulling from my purse my most recent lithium refill.

"Oh," she whispered, turning to look out the bay window.

FIFTY-FOUR

Jess

We talked for a good while. She told me about Donny, how he overdosed one night down in the field near the Horseshoe Curve. Same place where they had met and partied in high school, right where he proposed to her.

"No ring. He promised me one. Didn't have the money, though. Never did get it," she said.

New Orleans was the only trip they ever took together.

"This tattoo, that's like my wedding ring," she said, bouncing her leg up in the air.

He died before they got married. Karen was less than three months pregnant at the time. She never did tell him she was having a baby.

"Why didn't you tell him?" I asked. "He should have known," I said, as if it was okay for me to judge her in some way.

"I couldn't bring myself to do it. He was drunk half the time as it was. One day, he had a job, the next he got fired. Depressed constantly. Guess I should have known something was up the night he did it, but things weren't great between us and I was glad he was out. Gave me a break, you know?"

Sure, I knew. My mom was always telling people she needed a break from me.

"What do you mean, he did it?" I asked.

"Killed himself. Don't know if it was on accident or purpose," she said.

My mom would have corrected her grammar, I thought.

"We'll never know. Not that it matters, anyway," she said. "Took a bunch of his pills, drank a shitload, and went to sleep. That was it. Jerry went looking for him, found him right there, lying in the grass. 'Peaceful as day' he called it."

* * *

"It wasn't for a couple months after that I found out I was having twins. You and your sister," she said.

"I know who you meant," I said. Bitchy again.

FIFTY-FIVE

JB

By the time Jerry was finished with the story of how Donny died, with Ann interrupting now and again to fill in some gaps, Jess and Karen were back outside on the porch. Macy, whom I had not heard from in a while, appeared to be napping on the wicker rocker. The others had left.

"This has been nice," Jess said to no one in particular.

"You guys want to stay for a while? I can fix something to eat," Karen asked, arm on Jess's shoulder.

I was hungry and would have been fine with it, but Jess clearly was done.

"No. Thanks, though. It's late and we need to get going early in the morning. I really do need to get back home. See everyone before I get back down to work. It's a good ride back tomorrow, so, yeah, no, but thanks." She was struggling.

"So nice to meet you," Macy said. Popping up out of the rocking chair, shaking hands and hugging both Ann and Karen, all in one flawless, Olympic gymnast motion. Her legs. That smile. The way she handled everyone as if they were her family, too. She was beautiful, I thought. And just so young.

"All set, Jess?" she asked.

Jess nodded and leaned in to hug Karen once more.

"Let's roll, Uncle Bro," Macy said.

Nothing like a woman calling you "uncle" to bring reality to bear.

It was in that couple of moments, there on Karen's porch, that I really first noticed it. These two girls were not just friends. It was much more than that. They were connected, on the same plane, or whatever the cliché is. Jess wanted out, Macy knew it without a word between them. She steered the goodbye and took care of things so Jess wouldn't have to do it. Jess didn't have to say thank you. She appreciated it, I was sure. Aside from that, though, Jess expected it. She knew it. Macy was there. Macy would help.

I had that once.

FIFTY-SIX

Jess

We grabbed some coffee and yogurts from the complimentary lobby breakfast and took off.

I sat in the back again. I hadn't slept much, not that anything in the room at the Hampton Inn was uncomfortable. That wasn't it. It was strange, I thought. I was happy to have met her and learned about where I came from. It was sad about Donny, but more like a movie or TV show kind of sad. It was about someone else, not me. I was disconnected from those people, and meeting Karen, looking through the scrapbook, finding out about her and Donny, none of that really made much difference to me. I went into all of this, trying to find her, then deciding to meet her, thinking that it was going to mean something to me, change my life in some way. Make me better.

Now it was done. I knew who she was and what she looked like. As best as I could, I got it. Why she did what she did. Gave us away. No money, no place to live. Her mother, my grand-mother, would not let her stay home if she kept the baby. Babies. It wasn't really a choice for her. I understood. She did what she thought she had to do. "Played the cards she was dealt," my dad would have said.

But now it was done. I wasn't sure where I would go from here in terms of our relationship; although we "liked" each other on Facebook, exchanged email addresses, and promised to write, send pictures, stay in touch. Maybe even Snapchat or share Instagram pictures. All that crap. In the car and on the way home, somehow I didn't think any of that would happen. And, I thought to myself, that was okay. I wasn't angry. I wasn't happy. It was nothing.

* * *

A second four-hour trip in the backseat was fine with me. I really didn't want to talk anyway. That didn't seem to be much of a problem as Macy and Uncle Bro were chatting it up in the front seat, rehashing their time on the porch while I was inside with Karen, laughing a lot about Jerry.

"He probably wanted you to show him your Johnson. Prove you're a Jew," Macy said.

"Christ, that would have sent him over the edge. A Jew on his porch. A Jew lawyer at that. Wish I had some horns. Would have given him a heart attack," he said.

"That's coming for him, one way or the other," Macy said. "How the hell can he even stand up with that load in front? Looks nine months pregnant," she said. They both laughed.

"You should get that tattoo, Jess," Macy said, turning around toward me.

"How about you let her think about things before she permanently disfigures herself," Uncle Bro said.

I didn't care about waiting or thinking about anything. It seemed like the right thing to do.

"I will if you will, Mace," I said.

"Sure," Macy said, not hesitating. "It's got a cool meaning, plus I thought it was pretty," she said.

"What about you, Uncle Bro? You in?" Macy asked, punching him in the shoulder.

"No thanks, not me. Too scared of needles," he said.

"Uncle Bro, it hardly hurts and you can do a little one, like on your shoulder. Auntie Laurie would like it, I bet," I said, leaning forward and giving him a second bop in the shoulder.

"Hey, I'm driving, you two," he said, pretending to be annoyed. He liked the attention, especially from Macy, it seemed to me.

"There is no way I am doing it. I tried a couple of times, walking into some tattoo shops, but never had the guts to go through with it. Laurie has one. I like it on her, just don't think I could do it," he said.

"Your wife has one? Where is it?" Macy asked.

"Tramp stamp," I said.

Uncle Bro looked at me from the rearview mirror, an eyebrow raised, wondering.

"My dad told me," I said.

"Figures," he said, smiling.

FIFTY-SEVEN

JB

"Look at you, tough guy," Laurie said, admiring my new tattoo on my right shoulder.

"Like it? It's a fleur-de-lis. A symbol of perfection, life, and a bunch of other stuff." I couldn't remember exactly.

"Very sexy, yes. Get dressed. I'll take a closer look later. We have to get to the cemetery," she said, giving my ass a quick squeeze on the way to her closet.

* * *

There was nothing much to the cemetery service. While it is customary for Jewish people to have a ceremony unveiling the grave marker no later than a year after the death, Tom's was actually just a bit beyond the twelve months. It wasn't my business and I didn't care anyway. The rest of the boys were here, Tom's closest friends, his brother, Lianne and the girls. Having said my goodbyes a long time ago, I could have passed. I went because I had to. That was it.

I daydreamed during the few prayers, a short eulogy that Kasey read from some notes. Jess stood quietly next to her mom while her sister spoke, dressed plainly, no doubt more than a little too casual for her mother's taste, in some dark jeans and a leather jacket. When it was all done, we each laid stones on top of the marker, a tradition the rabbi reminded everyone meant to symbolize the fact that someone has visited the grave.

On the way out, I talked for a few minutes to Kasey and then Lianne. In black like her mother, Kasey thanked me for bringing up Jess from Florida.

"No problem, Kasey. Happy to do it. How are you and your mom doing?" I asked.

"Mom, she's doing well, I think. Made some new friends, goes out a lot. I moved home after finishing school. Working part-time while studying for my CPA exam," she said.

Her dad I know would be proud and I told her so, putting my hand on her shoulder.

"I do miss Jess, but I get why she had to leave. Best for all of us, probably," she said.

I know. I get it," I said, turning to Lianne.

* * *

"You got her here," Lianne said, wiping her eyes.

Not a thank you, just recognition that I had done what she asked.

"Happy to do it," I said, repeating myself.

"He would have wanted her here," she said.

"I assume you did, too," I said.

"It's fine and, yes, it is the right thing. Thanks for letting her stay at your house," she said.

We had plenty of room. Even though Jess had gone right to sleep the night before, it felt nice having a kid, Tom's kid, spending the night. She didn't want to stay at her old home, and even though I thought she should go see her mom and Kasey, it was not the time to push her.

"She doing okay? In Florida, I mean," she said.

"Seems like it, yes," I said. "To be honest, I'm glad you called. It's been great for me, too. Spending time with her, helping her out over the last few weeks."

Lianne looked at me. Irritated? Angry? Curious? Maybe some combination of the three.

One thing was clear. She knew nothing about Jess finding Karen.

FIFTY-EIGHT

Jess and Jamie

"It's so great to see you, Jess, come on in. Sit down. Like the new chairs?"

I liked the green leather ones, but these are nice, yeah."

"Want a fidget toy?"

"Funny."

"So, tell me all about it. I've been thinking about you since our phone call. You made it up to see her?"

"Yeah, it was okay. Found the place with no problem. My Uncle Bro and Macy came with me."

"Must have made it easier, I guess. To have them."

"Yes. I think so. Still weird anyway."

"What do you mean, weird?"

"I mean, I expected something, I just don't really know what it was. I did it, decided to find her. It all happened so fast. After all the years of thinking about her, I guess I had some picture in my head."

"You mean of how she looked or how she would be?"

"Both."

"And?"

"She's fat. They are all fat."

"Who is 'they all'"?

"Karen, her sister, everyone else that was there."

"What else?"

"I don't know. She's fat. That's pretty much it."

"Come on, Jess. We don't work that way. We've known each other too long. Except for her weight, what else can you tell me?"

"He's dead."

"Who?"

"My father, my biological father, I mean."

"Oh."

"Killed himself maybe. She's not sure. Could have been an accident, *but I don't think so. Was depressed. Mental illness. Bipolar, she says. Took a lot of pills. Sound familiar?"*

"Mental illness can be hereditary. You know that."

"Appears I drew the short straw, like always."

"It doesn't mean you will end up like him, Jess. You have a much better understanding of yourself than he probably did."

"Guess me and dads don't mix too well."

"One has absolutely nothing to do with the other, Jess."

"I mean, sure, I know, but really, two dead fathers?"

"That has to feel bad. I know it does. You worried you are going to start to cut again?"

"Maybe. Almost did before I came back up here. Before I went to meet her. Haven't thought about it though, since then."

"That's good. The 'not thinking about it' part. Can you tell me about Karen? Other than her weight, I mean."

"I know that wasn't right."

"What's she like?"

"She is nice. Simple, you know? Not dumb, I don't mean that. Has a job, some county government thing. Not a lot of money but does okay, I think. Has her own house. Works hard. Kind of strikes me as someone who just doesn't give up, no matter what happens, you know what I mean?"

"I do. Now that does remind me of someone."

"I don't know about that. I'm living in a little apartment, barely paying the bills. Pouring drinks and bouncing my boobs around for a buck or two tip."

"Bounce 'em while you can, kid. Tougher to do as you get older, trust me."

"Yours look fine."

"Okay, let's move on from the breast talk. How did you leave it with Karen? You going to stay in touch?"

"I don't know. She says she wants to come down to Florida some time, meet my friends, spend time with me. She has only been to a beach once her whole life. Crazy. She needs to save money for a ticket. Plus

166

where would she stay? With me, like she is my mom? Didn't give me away? I am supposed to let that all go? Forget about it?"

"No, you are not. You can try to understand it, though."

"I do. I guess."

"It's a lot—a tremendous amount—for anyone to take in, Jess. Think about it. Be fair to yourself. Try."

"Fair? What are you talking about? I am screwed. Two dead dads, one mom who gave me up, another who can't stand me."

"Jess, work with me a minute."

"Sure. Whatever."

"You know a girl. She's your age. Her dad died a year ago. She left home. Has a job, her own place. She's supporting herself."

"This is dumb."

"She's adopted. Has the courage to meet her biological mom. Asks questions she has wanted to ask since she was a little girl. Finds out her biological dad is dead, too."

"Yeah, and?"

"And? And? She's still standing up. Taking care of herself."

"What's the point?"

"The point? The point is—what do you think of that girl?"

"She's fucked up."

"Aside from that."

"Don't know."

"Be honest. What do you think of that girl?"

"I don't know."

"What do you think of her, Jess?"

"She's okay. She's doing okay."

"Exactly."

FIFTY-NINE

Jess

I've been in therapy for as long as I can remember. I understood what she was doing. To her, to anyone else, it looked like I was okay. And, maybe I was. All I know is that I didn't feel okay. I didn't know how to tell Jamie that there was nothing. I didn't feel anything. Not sad, relieved, fulfilled, nothing. When it was all done, I was on my way back in the car, like I was going to work or to lunch. That was it. One thing to the next.

I did my best to listen, to hear her. I really did. Not like when I was younger and I went because I had to, or sometimes anyway, basically because it was better than sitting by myself. She had drinks and snacks and for an hour I could say whatever I wanted without anyone being mad at me.

Now, though, it was different. I wanted to see Jamie. I wanted to talk to her. It was nice that I didn't have to pay, or didn't think I had to pay. Maybe she sent my mom a bill, but I doubt it. I told her all I could about meeting all of them and, God help me, made some stuff up about how it all "made me feel."

It was the strangest thing. I was apprehensive, anxious on the way up. Jamie asked what I was thought was going to happen, that I shouldn't get any ideas or have expectations of anything— I really don't think I did. I imagine most adopted kids want at some time to meet their biological parents. The questions, I assume, are pretty much the same? Why did you give me up? Why did you get pregnant if you didn't want me? Do you ever think about me? How could you do it? Send two daughters away? Stuff like that. Fact is that Karen answered those questions for me without my having to ask them.

That left for me to decide what to do about the whole session with my mom thing that Jamie suggested. She was definitely surprised that I had not told my mom about meeting Karen and doing everything that I did to find her, getting Uncle Bro involved and all that. Maybe I should have told her. Probably, yes, I should have. But she did not call me all year. Not even a call on my birthday, although I did get a gift card and short note wishing me a happy birthday and *"hoping it's a good year for you"* message. Of course, I didn't call her on her birthday. Mother's Day either.

I was not sure if I wanted to sit with the two of them for an hour—mom and Jamie. I had not sat alone with my mom for more than a few minutes since I was, I don't know, maybe eight or so. Not only that, but I didn't think she would come even if I did ask. Jamie said she would. Even if I was right, "doesn't hurt to ask," she said.

So, after an hour or so sitting at the cemetery with my dad, at his headstone, stacking pebbles inside the *O* in "Tom," I made a decision and called her.

She said yes.

SIXTY

Jess

"You better give Bobby a call. Wants to make sure we will be back to work tomorrow night," Macy said. "I told him, but I think he wants to hear it from you, too."

I missed Bobby. Although we didn't spend much time together outside The Wreck and were hardly even friends, I caught myself thinking about him in the last few days. His smile. How he trained me to bartend. His hand on mine the day before I left to come up north.

"Girl, you really need to wipe that 'wanna fuck that guy' look off your face. He is way too old for you and plus, he's like my uncle. It's a little gross, to be honest," she said.

"Really? And what about you and my Uncle Bro?" I asked. "Didn't think I noticed all that flirting at the bar, in the car?"

"The man is married and happy. Okay. Okay. I hear you. He is cute, though, in an old dude DILF sort of way," she said.

Macy peeled off her T-shirt and started dancing. Her hips curved and swayed, she pulled her hair back and made a breathy orgasm kind of sound. Nothing on top but her sports bra, she purred her best Rod Stewart, "If you want my body and you think I'm sexy, come on sugar dance with me. . . ."

That's why the girl killed it with tips, I thought.

"Jesus, Mace, put your shirt on. They are right upstairs," I said.

"Maybe a threesome—me, hunky Uncle Bro, and his hot wife with the tramp stamp," she said.

"You are crazy," I said.

She laughed.

"Put the fucking shirt on," I said.

* * *

"Hey, Bobby, it's me, Jess," I said. Now fully clothed, Macy was sitting at the kitchen table, her leg on top of my lap, listening to every word.

"You still coming back, right Jess?"

"Absolutely, yes. Uncle Bro has an extra car for me to use. I have a therapy thing with my mom in a little bit, and then we are going to see some friends later this afternoon. Uncle Bro is driving us to the airport after," I said.

"The uncle who's not really your uncle," he said.

"Yes, that's the one."

"Okay, good. I'll get you girls at the airport. Text me your flight info and just call me when you get off the plane," he said.

"You sure? We don't get in 'til around eleven. Busy time at the bar."

"No problem, Cary and Seeds can cover the kitchen. Got your buddies from the bike shop helping out also," he said.

"Really?"

"Yeah, just got to keep Kip in check is all, between that annoying gum thing he does and hitting on the women, not the best bartender I've ever had, but it worked out okay in a pinch," he said.

I hoped he didn't know about Kip and me. I scratched my crotch, half expecting the gum to still be there for everyone to see. Like that woman from the book I had to read in tenth grade. I couldn't think of the book or her name. They made her wear a big *A* on her chest. Hester Prynne. That was it.

"Well, I'm glad you got things covered when we were gone. And I do appreciate it. Your letting Macy come with me."

"No problem. I am glad you're coming back," he said.

"You didn't think I was going to come back?"

He didn't answer.

"You'll tell me how it went when I see you tonight, I hope," he said, seeming to mean it.

"Sure, if you want."

"I do, Jess," he said.

SIXTY-ONE

Jess

"She's in my chair," I said, to Jamie.

She and my mom both looked at me. I had been coming to this woman's office for a real long time, and I always sat in the same chair. Same spot, at least, until Jamie got new chairs. It was still my place, though, where I was supposed to sit.

"No problem, Jess, you take mine," Jamie said.

"That's your chair. You sit there," I said, pulling out the wooden chair from up against the wall.

"You asked me to come, Jess. So I'm here. Already you are mad and all I did was sit down," my mom said.

"I'm not mad," I said.

"Yes, you are," Jamie said.

Mom looked at me with that same look she had given me for all my years growing up. *I am right and you are not*, is what she said to me, without actually saying anything.

"And that's okay," Jamie said.

I shot mom back the same look.

She looked away, out the window.

"So, Lianne, it's been a long time. You look great," Jamie said.

That perked her back up.

"Thanks, Jamie," she said, crossing her legs and bouncing a new pink Nike over her knee.

"It's been a tough year, I am sure," Jamie said.

"You could say that," Mom said. "My husband died and my kid ran away, so yes, it's been kind of difficult."

"I didn't run away," I said.

"Okay, you're right, you didn't run away. You just left. Told me you were leaving and a couple of days later you were gone. Threw your clothes into a garbage bag and took off. Right after your father died," she said. "Same as always, do whatever you want, whenever you want. It doesn't matter what anyone else thinks or feels."

I'd heard this speech more than I cared to remember.

"Here we go again," I said.

"Hold on, Jess. Lianne, I hear you saying that you don't think that Jess cares about how her actions affect others. Is that what you mean?" Jamie asked.

"That's what I mean. Never has," she said.

"That's not true," I said, sitting up in my chair. My days of backing down were over.

"Give her an example of what you mean, Lianne. What has happened that makes you feel that way?" Jamie said.

"It seems like a waste of time to me. She's all grown up and it's done. In the past," my mom said.

"Maybe it is, but let's try anyway, Lianne. Tell her what you mean," Jamie said.

"How about when we were at the Kramer's house for Super Bowl. Remember that? You took that whole tray of food that Allison made and ran away with it. Went out back and tossed it in the grass, remember that?"

"What was I, eight?"

"Okay, how about a few years ago, you weren't eight then, we finally got invited to go away with another family, the Mayers. Your sister was so excited. Going down to their beach house for a long weekend. Would have been great. Could have been, I should say. But, no, not Jess. She won't go, locks herself in her room, screams, and throws a big tantrum. Play all over your dad's sympathies about it being Kasey's friend, not yours. Made him feel bad, so he stayed home with you."

"You went with Kasey, anyway. So what?"

"Just once, maybe we could have done something as a family. You just would never let us. Never," she said. "I would have liked to have been down there. Go to the beach, the boardwalk. Laugh and have fun. Like a normal family," she said.

"That's not true. We went places," I said.

"Not too much. And when we did, I had to spend all my time worrying about what you were going to do. Throw food, say something inappropriate, irritate your sister. God knows what. It never ended. Life on eggshells, that's what it was," she said.

"Maybe if you let me be sometimes, instead of telling me what to do every day, what to wear, how to act, it would have been better," I said. "Always had to control me."

"What do you mean, she had to control you, Jess?"

"I mean, every single thing. All day and even all night. Couldn't eat what I wanted."

"You would only eat junk," she said.

"Made me wake up an hour before Kasey every morning, just to take medicine."

"The medicine helped you be calm, focus better in school," she said.

"Made me sleep in my clothes I was going to wear the next day."

"That gave you more time to get ready for school," she said.

"Even on Saturdays. She made me get up early, get on that short bus to go with the adoption group."

"You didn't have any friends. I wanted you to have friends," she said.

"You were always trying to fix me, make me be different."

"I was. That's true. I wanted you to fit in. Get along. Waiting. Always just waiting for something to happen. I never knew what you were going to do or say," she said.

"You said that already."

"It's true. One minute, you would be talking, interacting with everyone, the next, who knows? Screaming, yelling, crying over nothing. Laughing too loud. Telling an adult to 'fuck off.' You were obnoxious."

"I hated when you called me that."

"I was trying to help you. I wanted people to like you," she said, her voice softer now.

I changed course.

"I could never do anything right in your eyes anyway."

"You could have. You just chose not to," she said.

"I just wanted you to love me is all."

"I did. I do. It's just hard to love someone who is always doing their best to make your life miserable," she said.

"The only way you ever paid any attention to me was if I did something to make you mad."

"Negative attention," Jamie said.

"Better than no attention," I said.

"Every day, I got up. Hoping it would be better. A new day. Promised myself I would be a better mom to you, that I would actually enjoy being your mom," Mom said.

"Never happened, though, did it?" I asked.

"No. Not too often."

"It did with Kasey, though," I said. "She was always perfect."

"She wasn't perfect. But she was easier. Sweet. Pleasant. She listened. Made her bed, cleared her dishes. Didn't talk back. What do you want me to say? She was a good kid."

"And I was a bad kid."

"It's not good and bad, Jess. The world is not painted in blacks and whites. Do you hear what your mom is saying to you?" Jamie asked.

"I guess, maybe. I was difficult. So what? That means she should be mad at me all the time? Not talk to me?"

"I think she is saying she loved you, but couldn't figure out how to be a mother to you," Jamie said.

"You just wore me out, Jess. Still do," Mom said.

"So why didn't you ever try to tell me all that? You hardly even said a word to me after dad died."

"That's not true. I invited you to go to dinner with us. Go to the mall. Things we did together."

"See what I mean?" I looked at Jamie. "Including me in things they do together."

Jamie nodded. "Lianne, you hear what she is saying?" she said, leaning forward, elbows on her knees.

"That's not what I meant," Mom said.

"I was always on the outside. In my room, punished, whatever. Watching you and Kasey do stuff. Stuff you two did together. Never asked me what I might want to do. Something you could do with me."

"Okay, so it's my fault that your sister was pleasant to be around. Still blaming everyone but yourself for your actions," she said, shaking her head.

"You just let me leave. You didn't care."

"I did care, I just had nothing to say. Whatever I would have said to you, what difference would it have made?" she asked, looking at me as if I knew the answer.

"If I asked you to wait and stay awhile, you would have fought with me anyway. I let you go because I had to. It was the right thing for all of us," she said.

We were quiet for a minute. She needed a break, I think, just like I did.

"Like it was the right thing for you to find Karen without talking to me about it first," she said, ending the lull.

"You know about that. Uncle Bro told you," I said.

"Yes, he told me. And it's fine, I knew you would want to know about her. Sooner or later," she said.

"And you're not mad?"

"You're too old for me to be mad at, to be honest. Same old thing with you, though. What you did, finding Karen. Didn't you stop for a second and think that there was someone else involved?" she asked.

"You?" I asked.

"Jesus Christ, Jess. Really?"

"Oh. Yeah. Kasey. I didn't think about it. About her. Sorry," I said.

"See?" she said, looking at Jamie now. "This is what I am talking about. What I've been talking about for years. She thinks about herself, does what she wants to do to. It doesn't matter who else gets hurt. Says she's sorry and it should all be fine," she said.

Jamie nodded. "Jess?"

I was crying. Scratching my arm. I was . . . I was sorry.

"It's not okay, but it is. Understand what I am saying?" Jamie asked.

"I think so," I said.

"Stop, Jess," my mom said, noticing my scratching. "Your dad hated when you did that." Touching the scars on my arm.

"Okay, I know," I said, remembering.

She grabbed a tissue from Jamie's desk.

* * *

After the session was over, we walked to my car.

"When are you going back?" she asked.

"Tonight."

"Want to come over for a while and hang out at the house? Talk about Karen?" she asked.

"Can't. Sorry. Macy and I are going to stop in and see our friends. Dr. Palmer's group. They are finishing up and having a get-together at his house."

"Okay, whatever, as you would say."

She touched my cheek and rubbed under my eye with her thumb.

I waited for her to say something more.

She didn't.

Neither did I.

She got in the car and drove off.

SIXTY-TWO

JB

"How was your re-entry?" Laurie asked, setting a lasagna on the table.

It was my first day back in the office after more than a week. For once, I had really stayed away. The advent of technology over the last few years has changed how I practice law. Aside from court appearances, I can now do all I need to do from just about anywhere, provided I have a computer and a phone. Of course, being able to work from anywhere cuts in the opposite direction if I am taking a few days' vacation. Last week, though, I did it. No afternoon client calls, no emails, no complaints from Pam about the paralegal who never got to work on time or grousing about people in the office for not putting their coffee cups in the dishwasher.

"It went fine. The usual. A quick deposition then had a lot of catching up to do. Nice to know I'm needed, I guess."

"How did the deposition go?"

"Fine, pretty basic for the most part. Did get a real laugh at the end though," I told her.

She poured herself a glass of sauvignon blanc from Hall Vineyards in Napa, from a case we ordered during a trip out west a couple of years ago. Usually, Laurie drinks an eight-dollar bottle from Safeway, twisting it open and closed during the week until it's done.

"Look at you. What's the occasion?" I asked.

"You were gone. Missed our date night," she said, sipping the wine, rubbing her bare foot along the inside of my calf.

I grabbed her foot and pulled it a little farther up.

"Let's hear the story first. I'm hungry," she said.

The girl could still flirt, even after all these years.

"I could use a laugh," she said, leaving her foot right where it

179

was.

"Okay, so you and I have talked about this case. Where my guy has some sexual issues. Not exactly over the plate in terms of his preferences," I said.

"What's that mean?" she asked.

"He likes getting beaten on a bit. *S* and *M* kind of stuff. Kicked in the balls, smacked around, that kind of thing," I said.

"Sounds like a keeper," she said.

"So, when his wife finds out that he has had this secret life for the last ten years or so, she's not too happy about it."

"Hard to believe," Laurie said, rolling her eyes.

"A prince, I know. Anyway, she asks him to leave, which he does, then after a few months, she starts making allegations about his abusing the kids, wants to keep him from them. See them only on a supervised basis. At one of those centers, where you go for an hour while a stranger, usually a retired cop, sits there with a magazine and keeps an eye on things then writes up a report after," I said.

"What's the basis for her saying he abused the kids?" Laurie asked, ever the therapist.

"They have two daughters. One twelve and one ten. Both girls got caught a few times masturbating. First the older one, then the younger one."

"What else?"

"That's pretty much it. They masturbate, but didn't until recently. He is a pervert, so therefore must have abused them. That's her case, really," I said.

"Sounds sticky."

"You're a funny one."

"I mean, really. That is ridiculous. Remember when Sarah used to try to ring one up on the grocery cart? Almost all kids masturbate," she said.

"I know. So, anyway, I take the deposition of one of the nannies, she is Hispanic, speaks broken English, but good enough so we don't need an interpreter. We swear her in, I ask her some basic questions. Name, where she lives, how long worked for the family. That sort of thing."

"Sounds exciting."

"Not much up to that point. I asked her, *'Ma'am, did there come a time when you observed Kristen masturbating?'*

'Yes,' she said.

'How many times?'

'Four. Four times,' she said.

'Where was she when you saw her?

'On the sofa, watching her shows,' she said.

'And what did you do when you saw her masturbating?'

'I gave her juice,' she said."

"I mean, can you believe it? Didn't tell her it was private, to stop, just gave her juice. Too funny," I said.

"Not enough Tropicana on the planet if it was you," Laurie said.

"Tell me about it."

"Okay, let's go," she said, pulling at my waist. "We can do the dishes after."

SIXTY-THREE

Jess

"So, look who's back." It was Jacob, the Sandalman, turning from a table in the front of the room that was covered in plastic. There were plates of food, desserts mostly, and the big jug bottles of soda. He was stuffing some sort of pastry into his mouth. "Couldn't miss the big bash, huh?"

There was some decorating done, in a fifth-grade sort of way. Crepe paper was taped around the classroom and a few balloons floated, long strings hanging, and were bouncing around the room.

"We asked them to come, Jacob," Dr. Palmer said.

It had been a year, but Dr. Palmer had not changed. His hair was still a little mussed and greasy, hanging over some 1970s-style glasses.

"I know we invited them, but it's a long way to come just for an end to the group party, Doc," Dylan said. He was sitting, same as he used to, chair turned around, leaning over the back. "No matter how fancy it is," he said.

"We didn't come just for you, Dylan," Macy said.

He didn't ask for an explanation.

"Nothing is ending. Everyone is moving on. It's a graduation party," Dr. Palmer said.

"Graduation from Asshole Island," Dylan said.

"My man, Penis Face," Jacob said, leaning against the table of food and smiling at Dylan. "We got to get off the island, so a new crop of assholes can get on. Time for us to go," he said.

"I wish you wouldn't refer to this group that way," Dr. Palmer said. "We have learned a lot about each other. No one here is an asshole," he said.

"Jacob's an asshole," Dylan said.

"Oh, yeah. Except for him," said Dr. Palmer, looking over at

Sandalman.

The three of them laughed.

Kyra walked up and hugged us both. "Great to see you two. I've been carrying the load with these morons since you left. Dr. Palmer wouldn't let me bring in any new girls," she said.

"You look great, Ky," Macy said, extracting herself from the group hug. "You guys do, too. It's good to see you all," she said.

"Hi, Macy. Hi, Jess," another guy said, extending his hand to shake ours. He was good looking.

"I'm sorry," I said, not recognizing him.

I looked at Macy. She was staring at him too, trying to figure it out.

"It's me, Kenny," he said.

"Gave up karate," added Jacob. "Someone told him he should be a model. Pretty isn't he?"

"Went from Bruce Lee to Levi's," Dylan said, shaking his head.

"Man wears nothing but skinny jeans. Got them in every fucking color. Scarves, he wears scarves too. Even when its eighty degrees outside. Weird dude," said Jacob.

"This coming from a guy who only wears Birkenstocks," Macy said.

Jacob took his right foot out of the sandal, wiggling his long hairy toes Macy's way.

"Leave him alone," Kyra said, coming to Kenny's defense. "He's found himself, just look at him. We should be proud," she said.

"He does look good," I said, smiling at Kenny.

"Oh, God, give us a break, you two. First, a jujitsu killer, now a fashion model. Next week he'll probably be a forest ranger or some shit like that," Jacob said. "And you," looking at me now, "still with the long sleeves I see. Still self-mutilating?" he asked.

"Fuck you," I shot back.

Not like the old days, just a quick flare.

"Sorry," I said to Dr. Palmer.

Dr. Palmer cut in. "That's enough, you two."

"I think he looks great," said Kyra.

"Me too," said Dr. Palmer, making a "way to go" fist and pointing it at Kenny.

"Thanks, Doc," Kenny said.

"Let's all grab something to eat and drink, sit down for a while," Dr. Palmer said.

We all pulled up some chairs into a makeshift circle. I was still glaring over at Jacob.

"Ignore him. Still a dick," Macy whispered.

"One's a dick, the other a dick face," I said, so only she could hear.

"What I would like to do," Dr. Palmer said, "is go around to everyone. Tell all of us what each of you learned the most about yourself this past year. Also, if you can get yourself to do it," he was tilting his head and looking at Jacob specifically, "say something about one of the others in the group. Something that person did that you thought was particularly difficult. Maybe something he should be proud of," he said.

"Maybe we can do show-and-tell, too," Jacob said. "I'll go get my pet turtle."

"Keep it up and you get a second year on the island, asshole," Dylan said.

"And even though they have been gone awhile, I am hoping that you two can participate also," Dr. Palmer said, ignoring the bickering and looking at Macy and me.

This time I agreed with Jacob. This was just stupid.

"Sure we will," Macy said, banging my knee with hers.

After an awkward silence, we were able to work around the room, starting with Kyra, who went on about how she was "more inside of herself" than she was a year ago. That led, of course, to Jacob offering to get inside her too, just to keep her company.

Dylan gave it a try, thanking Dr. Palmer and snapping a

couple of pictures of the two of them to post on Instagram. "I'll tag you, tell everyone that you are a registered sex offender," he said, grinning.

"You do that, Dylan," Dr. Palmer said, clearly enjoying himself.

Even Jacob participated, standing up to speak. "A year ago, I was an angry guy. Mad at everyone. Fought and called people names. I had no friends and couldn't get along with anybody," he said.

"And look at you now!" Dylan popped, clapping his hands together.

"Exactly. Great work, Doc," Jacob said, laughing along with the rest of us.

When it was my turn, I was quiet for a minute. "I am still alive. I even have a best friend. Sounds stupid, things most people don't think much about, like breathing. That's good enough for me. For now," I said.

* * *

When it was over, we exchanged some email addresses and phone numbers. Made sure to be Facebook friends, Twitter followers.

"I've got three thousand followers," Jacob said. "People love my tweets."

"Can't wait," I said, giving him a quick hug and turning to Dr. Palmer.

"It was great to see you. Thanks for having us back," Macy said.

"Yeah, me too," I said. "I liked coming every week."

He looked at us. I think he was trying to think of something insightful or profound. He looked at both of us. It felt like a proud uncle or big brother was standing there.

"You two. Take care of yourselves. Take care of each other," he said.

SIXTY-FOUR

Jess

Uncle Bro drove us back to the airport. I sat up front this time.

We listened to some Southside Johnny on the way.

"Dude's pretty funky," Macy said. "Like the raspy voice thing he's got going. How old is he?"

"Not sure. Sixty-something," Uncle Bro said. "Still plays and tours. Mostly smaller spots, but he puts on a great show. I saw he was going to be somewhere near you in Florida later in the year. You guys should go."

"Might be a little old or too white for me, Uncle Bro," Macy said.

"Both," I said. "My dad took me a couple times. I mean, I liked the music, but it was definitely mostly white people. A lot of bad dancing," I said.

"Old, like me, you mean?" Uncle Bro asked.

"That's what she meant," Macy said, from the backseat.

"You look younger. Much younger," I said.

"Nice try, Jess. Thought you would like to hear a little Southside before heading back," he said.

"Got some on my iPod, but thanks," I said. "Still know all the words to a lot of the songs. Listen to them now and again. Remember when you and dad used to play 'Love on The Wrong Side' and pretend you were blowing the horns?"

"Yeah. Still do that. By myself, though. Usually in the car so no one thinks I'm nuts. Here you go," he said, clicking it on.

That cool piano intro—"*doop doop de doop de doop de doop*"—kicked on just as we pulled into the lane marked DEPARTURES and up to the curb. Uncle Bro got out and grabbed our suitcases from the trunk.

I waited a minute or two, not wanting to miss my favorite line: "*You were gone when I needed you by my side . . .*"

For some reason, that lyric, the one that always made me think of my dad, this time, I was okay. I grabbed my backpack from the floor and got out of the car.

Macy was talking to Uncle Bro, leaning into his waist, back arched, her hands on his shoulders. He smiled at her while she talked, then, out of the blue she laid a big fat kiss on his mouth. A little longer than the usual polite kind, and as far as I could tell in the rain and glare of headlights, he kissed her back.

Macy caught me in a stare. "No big deal. Didn't kill anyone," she said. "Meet you inside," she said, bouncing into the building.

"I feel younger already," Uncle Bro said. He knew I saw them and I guess figured there was nothing he could say. I wouldn't tell anybody. He knew that. Plus, Macy was right. No one got hurt.

"Good for you, Uncle Bro," I said. "My gift to you."

"One time only," he said.

"I know. And I want to thank you for everything. I do. I don't know if I feel better or worse, but I'm glad I did it," I said.

"It's been good for me, too, Jess. Really. I was glad to do my part, to help. You and your dad," he said.

"I know," I said. "Love you, Uncle Bro. Gotta go."

* * *

I didn't want him to see me cry, so I pulled the handle from my suitcase and started rolling it with me away from the car.

"Jess, hold on," I heard him yell.

I turned back. He left the car door open and was jogging at me. He had something in his hand.

"Almost forgot. She gave me two, one for you and one for Kasey," he said, handing me an envelope.

"Thanks, Uncle Bro. For everything," I said.

I stuffed the letter in my pocket and followed Macy into the airport.

We waited about an hour before the plane boarded. I sat next to the window, Macy in the middle seat next to me.

"So, you going to open it?" Macy said, after we were up in the air for a few minutes.

"I guess."

"What are you waiting for?" Macy said.

I took a breath and looked at the lights fading below.

I opened it.

SIXTY-FIVE

JB

And off she went. The last few weeks were in my rearview mirror, along with the airport, and Jess.

As a lawyer, particularly a trial lawyer, I tend to think in terms of advocacy, my responsibility to maneuver, strategize, and get the best result I can for my client, often in a courtroom. "Do what I am paid to do" has been the way I have looked at it for as long as I can remember. What got lost for me was the other role, the counselor role. A lawyer that clarifies perspective, advises his client, uses his skills to help the client find a better way, whatever that may mean, given the situation.

It was that piece of the lawyer in me that I tapped to help Jess. Kept in some compartment and seemingly forgotten about for a long time, it was that set of skills that came unholstered when I starting helping my friend's daughter. And, in the time we spent together, it became increasingly clear to me that behind the tough "I'm on my own and can handle it" façade that she walled herself in, she was a young girl. Still a kid in so many ways.

I, of course, was a long way from being a kid. Kissing a twenty-something girl in public at the airport had a fleeting thrill and excitement to it, I had to admit. But that was it, a moment. Driving home through the rain, back to the woman that I loved and had built a life with, I was glad I had it, but also was fine that it wasn't going to happen again.

Clicking from one Southside tune to the next, singing along and rapping my wedding ring on the steering wheel with each beat, a crazy guy alone in a car, I felt something. Not the predictable "another day, another dollar" mantra I sleepwalked through over the past several years. It was a feeling I had with my wife, with my children, but now, I felt it about my job, my work.

Pride.

SIXTY-SIX

To my daughters—

Even though I am writing this, I don't know if I will ever see either of you to give it to you. When I found out that I was having a baby (I didn't know it was two until later), I was so happy. I loved your dad, even though he had his problems. We both worked, me at the catalog division at the JC Penney warehouse nearby. I drive a forklift and put stock away. I used to work retail, but the money was better in the warehouse and we needed the money. So, I learned how to drive the forklift. I am the only girl to work it.

I got my high school diploma and wanted to go for more school to study how to be a traffic controller for planes. Would have meant me going somewhere else for school, but then me and your dad got serious and I decided to stay around. Plus my mom didn't have no money and we sometimes ate canned spaghetti for a few days in a row if she was out of work. My mom, your grandma, raised us alone. Her name was Shirley. My dad, your grandpa, his name was Bill, died when I was young. Some kind of trucking accident up in the mountains. Mom never liked to talk about it, so that's all I ever knew.

Anyways, I got pregnant and me and your dad, Donny, was going to stay at the house with mom and raise the baby there until we could afford to get our own place. But then he died, and that was that.

Once Donny was gone, I didn't know how I was going to pay for a baby. Then after I got sick one night, the ambulance took me to the hospital for some tests and they said I was having two babies.

Mom was sick over it, but she told me we there wasn't no way we could support one, much less two, especially with me not working, so I did what I had to. I decided to give you both up to a good home. I found an advertisement in the local paper where rich people are looking for babies, so I gave a call and talked to a lawyer. I told her no way would I split you two up, so she had to find me a family that wanted two babies.

I got to meet your parents after about five months. They drove up and we ate a nice lunch at the diner in town. I was so hungry. I ordered

190

the meat loaf double plate. They must have thought I had not eaten in a week. Tom told me to have whatever I wanted, so I did. He was real chatty and laughed a lot so I took to him right away. Lianne was quiet and not a real friendly type, but I figured with that man as your dad, you girls would be in good hands. He had a good job and I was sure you would be okay and have a life you couldn't get here with me. So I signed the papers and they paid for all my doctor's appointments and some food until I delivered you babies.

In the hospital, I got to hold you both after you was born. Only for a little while, because I was afraid I would get too attached and change my mind. You spent most of your time in a little room that the lawyer arranged for Tom and Lianne to have in the hospital. After that first time holding you, I decided it was better for me not to see you again, so I didn't. When they let you guys go with Lianne and Tom, both of them came to say bye in my room. Tom thanked me and Lianne was crying when they said goodbye.

I was crying too and I thanked them for taking care of you girls.

I know it must be a bad thing to think I gave you away or maybe didn't love you. I loved you both. I just had to do it. I'm sorry and I hope you understand.

Love,

Your mom, Karen

P.S. I am writing this two times, so each of you gets one and it says the same thing.

SIXTY-SEVEN

Jess

Bobby was at the airport like he said. Not waiting in the cell phone lot for a call, he was right there when we came out past the security. Jeans, boots, snug white T-shirt. The usual. Nice.

I sighed as we walked toward him.

"Thanks for coming, Bobby," Macy said. "I need a drink. Know where I can get one?" she asked, giving him a quick hug.

"Think I can manage that," he said. "What about you, Jess?"

Looking at me now.

I was tired. Sad? Possibly. Relieved, too, that the whole thing was over. I read her letter maybe six times on the plane. I wanted to go home, get in my bed, have a drink, and try to sleep.

"If it's okay, I'd rather go back to my place, get some sleep before work tomorrow," I said. I knew I would be back on the schedule, probably not seeing any days off for a while.

* * *

"You sure, Jess? Might be better for you to be with some friends and throw a few back first, don't you think?" Macy asked.

She looked at me in that way she has. Her brows crunched together, forehead wrinkled. The "pug face" I call it.

Worried.

"You probably shouldn't be alone," she said.

I knew what she was thinking. Truly, I had not thought about cutting.

"I'll be fine," I said. "Really. Don't worry."

"It's no problem. Mace, I'll drop you off at the bar then run Jess home. Take five minutes," Bobby said.

I caught him looking at me. Staring? I couldn't tell, but doubted it. I felt run down, and was afraid I looked that way, too.

"You sure? I am fine. Don't need a chaperone," I said to Bobby.
"I'm sure," he said, grabbing my suitcase from my hand.

SIXTY-EIGHT

Jess

He offered to carry my stuff in. I didn't object.

"You need to get to the bar. Go ahead and thanks for helping me in, getting us at the airport," I said, flipping on the kitchen light and turning to walk him out.

"No, we're okay tonight. A little slow," Bobby said. "You want me to go?"

"No, it's okay. You can stay if you want."

"Macy said you could use some company."

"Don't know. Maybe. I do need a shower. Hate that airplane gross, grimy feel, you know?"

"Sure, I'll grab a beer, see what's on," he said, heading over to my fridge. "Take your time."

"Plenty to drink. Help yourself. Some tequila and Jack in the cabinet there," I said, pointing to where I kept my liquor.

"Perfect," he said, as I closed my bedroom door between us.

* * *

Usually I would have taken a long hot bath, but with Bobby in the other room, I didn't want him to wait. I didn't want to wait either. I washed my hair, shaved my legs.

I hoped he couldn't tell that I wanted anything, even though I was sure I did, so I put on some long boxer shorts and a baggy sweatshirt.

"Got you a glass," he said, as I sat down on the couch next to him, crossing my legs, Indian style.

"What you watching?" I asked, filling my glass with Jack Daniels.

"Discovery Channel. Shark Week reruns. You don't get HBO or Showtime?" he asked.

"No. Don't watch that much TV. It's pretty expensive," I said.

"No problem. I like watching these dudes hunt sharks," he said, resting one boot on my coffee table, not taking his eyes from the television.

I leaned back into the beige velour couch that came with the apartment. *Wonder how many people have sat, napped, maybe fucked on this couch*, I thought to myself.

There was about half a cushion between us.

"Hey, Jess, I, um, wanted to tell you. I . . ."

I cut him off and leaned my head into his chest, erasing the inches of distance between us.

"You like me," I said, looking at the TV.

"I do, yeah. I do," he said.

I could feel his breath, warm, on my forehead.

SIXTY-NINE

Jess

He picked me up, carried me into the bedroom. Really picked me up, cradled and carried me, like in a movie. We still hadn't kissed. Neither of us said a word.

Setting me down at the side of the bed, he raised my arms above my head and pulled the sweatshirt over and off. With the air-conditioning broken as usual, the ceiling fan was blasting away. He put his hands around and cupped my breasts, pulling me into him. I went to turn, tried to face him. Bobby held me there, not letting me swing around. He reached down, both hands into my shorts.

I wanted him, right then. No waiting, like all the other times I had been with other guys. In, out, fuck me, sometimes two or three times if I was really buzzed, then hit the trail.

His hands between my legs, massaging me with both, I started to feel differently. Maybe it wasn't a race, I thought. What's the rush?

I wanted to see him, look into those eyes. Take off his shirt, feel his chest, his shoulders, the muscles in his back. Do things to him, slowly too. But he held me in the same place, turned from him, even as my legs started to tingle, my breaths getting shorter, faster.

Maybe he didn't want to see me. See my face, I thought. Just do what he wanted. No emotion. That was a lot easier if you were looking at the back of someone's head, I thought.

"I'm in love with you, Jess," he whispered, kissing my cheek, fingers still rubbing me below.

"Sure you are," I said, quietly, sarcastic, disconnected and aloof as ever. Trying to be, anyway.

"I am," he said, turning me around, his hands now on my waist, guiding me onto the bed.

He stood above me, unbuttoned his jeans and peeled his shirt off, a small amount of sweat on his chest. Strong, firm, a shade more around his midsection than the other guys I had been with.

Not a boy.

A man.

"You can't love me," I said, pulling him down and into me.

SEVENTY

Jess

He didn't ask to stay, which was fine.

No way I was going down the "I love you" path, even with him, a guy I have been watching and wanting, mostly since I first saw him outside his place at The Cove. I knew better than that.

Sure, it was nice that he said he loved me, but he's not the first guy to do it, especially at that particular moment. So, no, no thanks, not interested. I am fine by myself, we can hook up as much as you want, Bobby, but that's it. No dinners, long talks, holding hands. I was meant to be alone. I knew that.

Before work, I took a walk out along the beach, for the first time in at least a month, maybe two. There were a couple of guys in wetsuits trying to surf the dinky waves. That made me laugh to myself, remembering my dad who loved to body surf and would go out in big monsters at Bethany Beach and Ocean City during our summer vacations. Scared the shit out of my mom who was sure he was going to kill himself. She would tell him, "If you hear your neck snap, stay down." I sometimes thought she was joking, sometimes not.

It was one of those typical Florida mornings. A little breeze, the sun was bright but not too hot yet. That, I knew, would come later. Macy wasn't due to be at the bar until five, and she loved the scorching hot late afternoons. I knew she would be outside maybe a couple of hours before work, lounging in nothing but a thong and bra, sipping an iced coffee. "Couldn't work this job without the 'caf' shot," she would say to whomever was around.

I took a break, sat in the sand. They were so different, Karen and my mom. Karen was this giant woman whose clothes were too tight, loved to hug, and couldn't get enough of me. My mom, on the other hand, preferred an air kiss and was a perfect fit in everything I could see. Except for me.

I decided right then that I should call her. Not now, but soon. My mom.

SEVENTY-ONE

Jess

"Jess, everything okay?" she asked right away.

Was she worried about me?

I sat down on my bed, folding the pillow under my head.

"Hi, mom. No, everything is fine. I just wanted to talk for a minute. Ask you something," I said.

"Okay, what's up?" she asked.

I thought about telling her about Bobby. How we got along and he was nice to me, respected me, and I did like him, but no, nothing too serious. I decided not to. That wasn't why I called anyway.

"Did Kasey read the letter? From Karen?" I asked.

"She's not like you, Jess. Not always searching for something better, different," she said.

"That's not what I meant," I said.

Not off to a good start, I thought to myself. A mistake to call. Definitely.

"Okay, no, Kasey has not seen the letter yet. Said she was not ready to read it," she said. "Sorry."

Sorry? Could not remember her saying that to me before. Ever.

"I was just wondering, what you thought of her when you met her. Karen," I said.

"It's been a long time, Jess. I guess I thought she was a young girl who was poor who had made some bad decisions and was trying to make the right one. I mean, I didn't make, sorry, I would have made a different one," she said.

"You would have made a different what?" I asked. "Decision?"

"I did, yes," she said. "I made a different decision."

"What are you talking about?" I asked.

"I guess you're old enough to hear it. Not something I am

proud about," she said.

"I don't understand," I said.

"When I was in high school, I got pregnant. I had an abortion," she said. "I didn't tell my parents, wasn't going to tell them. But I had some bleeding afterward and got really sick. Pops had to take me to the hospital. Something happened during the abortion. My uterus was damaged and I could never have any more of my own children."

"I'm your own child," I said.

"You are. Kasey, too. I misspoke. Sorry," she said.

"Yeah, okay," I said, not wanting to make an issue.

"Do me a favor, would you, Jess? Keep this to yourself. Kasey doesn't know and it's my story to tell her. Not yours," she said.

"I understand," I said.

"Anyway, your dad and I. We never really discussed it after. Once we got married, he really wanted children and since I couldn't have them, the only way was to adopt," she said.

"What about you? Did you want children?" I asked.

Quiet. A pause before she said anything.

"I was happy, Jess. Just the two of us. We went out, enjoyed ourselves. I didn't want that to change," she said.

"Oh," was all I could say.

That explains it, some of it. She never really wanted kids. Start with that, then add me and all my shit to the mix. No wonder she hated me, I thought.

"I thought God was punishing me for what I did. The abortion," she said. "That sounds awful and I know you won't like it, but that's what I felt. You were my punishment. I got what I deserved, for killing my baby," she said.

And I thought I was fucked up.

I was feeling sick. Rubbing my arms. I started toward the bathroom. That feeling. It was back.

"You still there, Jess?" she asked.

"Yeah, I'm here," I said, reaching into the medicine cabinet.

SEVENTY-TWO

JB

"That motherfucker," Lisa Torrance said, leaning forward in one of my turquoise leather client chairs from across my desk, her pink blouse unbuttoned one spot lower than what might be considered appropriate in the business world. I tried not to notice, "tried" being the operative word.

When I got back from Florida, I decided to ditch the stodgy oak wood and brown lawyer office for a brighter, more colorful and modern look. The husky old desk and worn credenza were replaced with a contemporary metal and glass top worktable and a funky wood piece that Laurie found on one of her jaunts to a local roadside antique store. The topper was a bright orange leather couch that gave the whole office a very 1960s, retro feel. I had the office painted in a brighter eggshell-like color with a gold accent wall, and got myself one of those expensive Herman Miller Aeron chairs. I felt like a pilot.

Lisa was one of my favorite clients. She always listened attentively and, unlike many others paying me for it, regularly followed my advice. Blonde, tall, and with a wholesome and bright Ralph Lauren cover girl smile, she reminded me of a line from the theme song to the old *Mary Tyler Moore Show*: "Who can turn the world on with a smile?"

Married to a high-wage earner for almost twenty years, her kids grown, Lisa was trying to navigate her way back into the workplace. No matter what job she found, however, Lisa's income would never be anywhere close to that of her husband, a partner with a large DC law firm, who handled massive, multi-billion dollar anti-trust cases. In my divorce lawyer world, that meant that there was an "unconscionable disparity" between the two in terms of their abilities to earn, and as a result, Lisa was a candidate for long-term, if not indefinite, alimony.

Although there was a house in Bethesda, some retirement money, and a few assets to debate about and fight over, the real dispute in the case was over the amount of alimony that Lisa's husband would have to pay and for how long he would have to pay it. Jackson, her husband, whose name I couldn't say without rolling my eyes, wanted to be done with Lisa as soon as possible and, of course, pay her as little as possible.

Neither Lisa nor Jackson wanted to litigate the case, so his lawyer and I had spent the last several months negotiating a financial agreement, exchanging redlined drafts back and forth via email. Ultimately, it was only the alimony provision that remained unresolved and standing in the way from Lisa extricating herself from a marriage that from the sounds of it, her side of the story anyway, was never a happy one.

Some states have alimony guidelines, a legislative creation that provides a calculation designed to determine a "recommended" alimony award once various information about a given case is entered into a software program. Things like ages of the parties, how much each person earns, how long the parties have been married, that sort of thing, is all entered into the "calculator" and the guidelines program spits out a recommended award in terms of amount and duration of the alimony payment. Designed in part to take away a lot of a judge's discretion, not necessarily a bad thing, many states now have alimony guidelines that the trial courts are to follow. Also, these guidelines are supposed to alleviate the wide variations in alimony awards in cases where circumstances, at least on paper, seem similar. The problem with alimony guidelines is that they don't take into account the real-life issues and events that occur during a marriage and can, or should at least, impact the amount of alimony to be paid. Things like how long someone has been out of the workplace, how long it will take that person to become retrained or able to learn a certain skill, what kind of bastard a fifty-five-year-old husband might have been who, on a whim, simply decided to take off and move in with his twenty-five-year-old girlfriend. And what about the guy who has earned hundreds of thousands of dollars for years, but now for no real reason other than he decides to slow down, work and earn less, and as a result, not coincidentally, is unable to pay as much alimony as he would if he hadn't resigned as a partner from the accounting firm to start that non-profit or bait-and-tackle store down in the Keys? Alimony Guidelines don't have a box for that.

Thankfully and appropriately, Maryland has yet to adopt or require the application of any alimony guidelines formula. That means, in the event of a trial, judges can hear more about just numbers in terms of current income, but also the other, sometimes, nonfinancial factors relative to the breakup of the parties' marriage that might be relevant.

Once alimony has been awarded, usually as part of a divorce decree, it is modifiable or ends only when the Court itself or the parties themselves agree to do so, absent the existence of what is called a terminating event. In other words, what can happen that automatically causes alimony to end? In Maryland, the only automatic terminating events, absent a written agreement between the spouses to the contrary, are death of either party or if the spouse who is receiving the alimony gets remarried.

In a case like Lisa's, the spouse making the money, Jackson here—just has to be a douchebag with a name like that—looks for potential ways in which he can add terminating events to a settlement agreement. Often, people in his position want to include some provision that calls for a possible modification or termination of his alimony payment in the event his income drops substantially, possibly due to termination from a job or disability. This type of provision, sometimes referred to as a catastrophe clause, is not uncommon and any divorce lawyer advising a high-wage earner who does not at least discuss pushing to include something along these lines in an agreement is simply not doing his or her job.

Another popular provision for a person paying alimony is the desire to include a cohabitation clause that can also serve to trigger termination of an alimony obligation. In other words, if the recipient of the alimony ever begins living with someone else, then the alimony payments end.

After agreeing upon the amount of alimony that poor Jackson was going to send to Lisa each month, it was the language to be included in the cohabitation clause that led to more negotiating between myself and Jackson's lawyer.

So, with Lisa across my desk, I laid out for her what it was he wanted.

"He is looking for a provision that will make it so he does not have to pay alimony if you decide to live with someone. In a romantic relationship, I mean. Not a roommate or tenant thing, just if you have a boyfriend," I said, before she cut me off.

"Or girlfriend," she said, smiling at me.

I tried not to spit my coffee out.

"Okay, significant other. If you live with someone in a romantic relationship, he doesn't want to have to pay to support the two of you, that's where he is coming from," I said, composing myself.

"Okay, I get that, but what exactly does he want it to say?" she said.

"Here is the provision that his lawyer proposed," I said and read it to her.

"In the event that Wife lives with any person with whom she has a romantic and sexual relationship for 180 overnights at her primary place of residence in any consecutive 365-day period, then Husband's alimony obligation shall terminate."

Reading that to Lisa was what got me the "that motherfucker" response.

She sat back in her chair and looked at me.

"So what do you think?" she said. "I put up with that asshole for twenty years, raised the kids, cleaned up, and cooked for him.

No movies, no nights out, vacations, nothing. A trip to his parents' beach house every summer. Woohoo. That's it. Dinner, TV, bed—that was our social life. Sex once a month maybe, missionary by the way. Maybe two minutes tops. So now, if I find someone, I have to give up the money—money it seems to me that I earned, too," she said.

"I don't disagree with anything you are saying," I said, wondering again what was wrong with the guy. Two minutes, once a month? He was mentally ill, I was sure.

"But, here's the thing, Lisa. Proving a romantic relationship is not all that easy, plus confirming one hundred eighty nights is a lot of paying an investigator to watch your house to see who is sleeping over. The rest of the deal works and this lets you move on," I said.

"I hear you, I do," she said, looking past me and out my window.

I let her think for a few seconds. "So what you want me to tell his lawyer?" I asked.

"Tell him I'll sign," she said.

"I think that's the right thing, considering the rest of the agreement," I said. "I will call after you leave."

"And one more thing I want you to make sure she tells her client," she said.

"Sure, what's that?"

"Tell her to tell my husband that I hope I go out and get fucked 179 nights in a row."

Hard not to like this woman, I thought.

And on a day like this, hard not to like the job either.

SEVENTY-THREE

Jess

"What the fuck, Jess?" Macy was upset. She knew.

"Nothing. I was cold is all," I said, turning away and walking back to the kitchen after finishing the table setup. It was 11:30 in the morning, 92 degrees already, and the bar opened in an hour.

She followed me toward the kitchen. "It's hot as shit outside and you have your long sleeves on. I know what that means. Goddam it, Jess, I thought you were done with that," she said.

I turned to face her as I approached the swinging door with the peeling sign that read "employees only."

Bobby was sitting at the table against the wall, having coffee. He was over again last night, as he had been now almost every night the last couple of weeks. He looked up at me.

"Hey, Jess. You all right?"

"I'm fucking fine, yeah," I said. "Can't we fix this sign already? It's been half falling off since I got here."

I was fourteen again, telling my mother to fuck off.

Bobby didn't say anything.

Macy grabbed my arm and started pulling at my sleeve.

"She's cutting herself again. You got to be fucking kidding me. I used up my vacation, spent all that time going to some godforsaken place in Pennsylvania for you. And you do this? Again? I could have been in Mexico or the Bahamas or someplace other than Pitts-fucking-burgh, that's for sure. Drinking and dancing." She was pissed. Ranting and pointing at me with one hand while her other was clamped tightly on my wrist.

"Stop," I said. "Just stop." I dropped my arms to my sides, energy gone.

"I just can't believe you. That you would do this," she said, crying now.

She dropped my arm and walked out.

207

I didn't move. Just stood there, facing the broken sign. Thinking it held some sad, pathetic meaning for me.

Back again. Left alone, in my room.

"Jess," Bobby said, wrapping his arms around my waist.

I pulled his hands from my waist and backed away, not looking at anything but the floor.

"Just. Just, don't," I said, walking out and into the parking lot.

Kip was pulling up on a bright red racing bike, on what was likely another morning test ride.

"Jess, what you think of this one? Pretty, huh?"

"Put on a fucking helmet. Going to kill yourself one day, moron," I said, blowing past him.

"What's got you twisted up first thing, Jess?"

Just leave me the fuck alone. Why can't people just leave me alone? I thought but didn't say, as I started to run back toward The Cove.

"No helmet law in Florida, anyway," he hollered at me.

I quickly turned, still running, and gave him the finger.

He looked at me, not saying anything.

Crack, crack.

SEVENTY-FOUR

Jess

"You want to talk about it?"

Macy and Bobby found me, in my chair, on the beach.

After leaving The Wreck, I went home, threw on a bathing suit, grabbed a chair and a couple of beers, and walked over. It wasn't hard to find me, I guess.

"Not really, to be honest," I said, staring out at the ocean from behind my new pair of Maui Jim's that I bought a couple of weeks ago from the Sunglass Hut at the mall. I looked at it like I earned something for myself, having been through the meeting with Karen, and my trying to make things better with my mom.

"Well, we're going to talk anyway, Jess, whether you want to or not," Macy said.

I looked at Macy, who was looking back at me. Bobby was not.

It was humid and the mist from the ocean fogged my glasses a little, but I left them on. I didn't want Macy and Bobby to see that I had been crying.

"She hasn't even called me," I said. "Karen."

"You expected her to call? Why?" Macy asked.

"I thought she wanted to have a relationship with me. I found her. We had that time together. I thought she would want to get to know me," I said.

"She went twenty-three years without trying to get to know you, Jess," she said.

"Can't blame her for that, I guess," I said, feeling sorry for myself.

"Here we go again. Poor Jess. She's adopted, her dad died. Only one in the world to get handed a few bad things," Macy said, mocking me.

"That's not it. You know that. It just doesn't seem right, is all. I pull my ass together, and after all these years, go find her. She shows me some pictures and we hug and that's it?"

"That's it. Yes. Right. Move on," she said.

"All that time I waited. Wondered what my mother would be like. I go find her. I do it. She doesn't lift a finger. Now, she can't even call me?"

Bobby broke his silence.

"You have a mother," he said. "Lianne. She's your mother."

I didn't say anything. Macy leaned back in the sand, her head into mine.

"And you have friends. You have Macy. You have me," Bobby said. Looking right at me now.

He reached into my lap and put his hand on mine.

"Oh, shit. No way," Macy said, noticing our holding hands, smiling at both of us.

SEVENTY-FIVE

Jess

"See you at the bar," Bobby said, pulling on his jeans while heading out of my apartment.

Since our talk on the beach a couple of weeks ago, I was feeling better. Work was good. Busy. Macy and I were back to laughing it up all the time, running the usual daily contest over who could make more in tips. Once work was done, I went to Bobby's or he came to my place. Some nights we slept together and didn't even have sex, which at first was very weird to me, but after a few nights of it, got to be comfortable. Warm. Right.

"Okay, sounds good," I said, as he was shutting the door.

* * *

I decided to call my mom again.

"Hi, Mom, it's me, Jess," I said.

"Hi, Jess. Everything okay?"

She asked that again. I liked it.

"Yeah, everything is fine. Just wanted to say hi, see how you guys were doing," I said.

"We're good. Started working this week. Got my certifications and teaching different exercise classes up at the gym."

"Very cool. Congrats," I said. I was happy for her. "What about Kasey?"

"She's doing well, interviewing still. Waiting to hear if she passed the last part of the CPA test," she said.

"I know I was hard," I blurted.

"Yes, you were," she said, but not in the usual angry way. More agreeable. Accepting.

"Why'd you do it?" I asked. "The abortion."

I heard her sigh. Sit down maybe.

"I was a kid. Seventeen. We both wanted to go to college, to school, all the stuff our friends were going to do. What was I going to do with a baby?"

"I don't know. Could have had the baby, placed it for adoption like Karen did," I said.

"That wasn't the right thing for me. Or your dad. It was what we had to do back then," she said.

"I understand," I said, thinking to myself about these two women, connected by my sister and me but such different people. Such different decisions.

"Have you talked to Karen at all?" she asked.

"No, she hasn't called me. I haven't called her either," I said.

"Oh. You okay with that?" she asked.

"Yeah, I am. I already have a mom," I said.

"You do. And you have enough trouble with that one," she laughed.

* * *

After a few minutes on the phone, we said our goodbyes and I promised to stay in touch. I still didn't mention Bobby.

Since I had a couple of hours until I had to be at work, I decided to stay in bed. I pulled the covers back over me and opened my legs, touching myself just a little.

After a moment or two, it came.

Not an orgasm.

I ran to the bathroom and threw up.

SEVENTY-SIX

Jess

The tests, all six of them, came up either blue or with a plus sign. Whatever. Both meant the same thing.

I couldn't tell Bobby. I decided to wait to tell Macy. My mom, she would have had a heart attack. I could have called Jamie, but decided it was time for me to stand up, handle something on my own for once.

Bobby gave me the afternoon off. I didn't tell him much, just that I wasn't feeling great and needed a few extra hours of sleep. Being a Wednesday, he wasn't worried about getting by without me during the daytime.

A couple of nights earlier, I went on line to find the closest Planned Parenthood location so I could go in and talk with someone who didn't know me and could talk about the options, without judging me or having any interest in what decision I made. When I went on the website for the West Palm location, I had to check a reason for my visit and there wasn't one that said "pregnant with questions" or something like that.

Pregnancy test? Didn't need that.

Morning after pill? Definitely too late for that.

STDs? I was always careful.

Abortion? Not ready for that one.

Thankfully, there was the "other" box. I checked that one and scheduled my appointment for eleven.

* * *

From the outside, the place itself was plain and not at all noticeable. It could have been anything—a health food store, even a used clothing store like the one where I worked at home. Just another store in a shitty strip center, really. It was brown

213

brick and had a sign that said, PLANNED PARENTHOOD OF SOUTH FLORIDA AND THE TREASURE COAST. The sign had a hole in the lower right corner where it looked like someone had thrown a rock through it. Nothing you could see from the outside indicated that there were women getting abortions or being treated for STDs or whatever else they did in there.

Inside was more of what I had expected. Bright white lights, one of those old dropped ceilings with the graying tiles; many were stained or broken and needed to be replaced. There were about ten chairs off to my right, filled with women, some clearly pregnant, others with kids already. A skinny, very pale looking woman was behind the C-shaped desk, sitting just high enough for me to see her face, but not much else. I signed in and told the woman that I had already taken the home tests and knew I was pregnant.

"They're not always right," she said.

"Oh, okay," I said, thinking, maybe it was a mistake. Hoping.

"Not usually, but sometimes," she said.

"How many tests you take?" she asked.

"Six," I answered, filling my information onto the clipboard form.

She looked up and wrinkled her lip, taking away my optimism.

"Well, probably not then. Anyway, we need to be sure before you can meet with the counselor. Check the box for the blood work. We'll do that now. Lab is here, so we can call you with the results and you can come back or you can wait an hour or so and we will have them for you. Just need to push your appointment back a bit if you decide to stay," she said, looking at her computer screen.

I had the blood work done, was able to push my appointment back to 2:00 pm, and walked around the shopping center for a while, grabbing two slices and a Diet Coke from Sal's Italian Express. While I was out, I texted Bobby that I needed until 6:00

pm, but was fine, just wanted to rest, nothing to be concerned about, missed him, and anything else I could think of to say so he wouldn't worry.

I came back in a little before my appointment, and the lady told me the counselor was ready for me. She got up from behind the desk and pointed at a white door.

"Go ahead in, third door on the left. Cheryl will be in to see you in a few minutes, once she is done with the one-thirty," she said.

I did as I was told, found a room with a round table that reminded me of the ones we had in kindergarten, just a little taller. There were four chairs around the table. The walls, like everything else in the place, were white, plastic-framed pictures of seashells on three of them, windows with the blinds pulled on the fourth.

After a couple of minutes of looking at my phone, trying to keep busy, a redheaded woman walked in, extending her hand to me.

"Hi, Jess. Nice to meet you," she said. "I'm Cheryl, the counselor here."

She was pretty, her hair all in place, slacks, heels, and a white blouse.

"Hi," I said, shaking her hand.

"So, you are pregnant, Jess. After six HPTs, you probably knew that anyway," she said.

"Had a feeling, yeah," I said.

She pulled out a calendar and I did my best to figure out the dates of my last period. From there, she was able to tell that I was between eight and ten weeks along.

"So, let's talk about your options, make sure you understand everything," she said.

"Yeah, okay," I said, breathing kind of heavy. Even though I knew the answer coming in, it was still not right, hearing a stranger tell me.

"First, of course, you can have the baby and keep it," she said. "Do you know who the father is?"

"Yes."

"And what does he think?"

"He doesn't know yet. I wanted to be sure."

"Well, now you are. Sure, I mean."

"So you think I need to tell him?"

"You don't need to decide that today. Let's stick to what you do need to think about."

"Like keeping the baby?"

"That's one choice, absolutely. And if you decide to do that, we can help you with a doctor, make sure you get prenatal care and all of that."

"I have health insurance."

"Great. Finding a doctor will be no problem. Do you already see a gynecologist?"

"No."

"That's fine. We can find you one near where you live."

"Okay, let's talk about the other choices," I said, resting my chin in my hand.

"You can have the baby, place her, or him, for adoption," she said.

"How does that work?"

"Again, we can help you speak with a non-profit group that helps match pregnant mothers with parents who want to adopt. Catholic Charities is one, and they have an office not too far from here. There are also private adoption agencies who will work with you to find parents for your child."

"I'm adopted."

"Well, good, then it's not a foreign topic for you. I have a lot of information I will give you to read when we are done. You can look at the different ways to place your baby for adoption, see what might work best for you. Again, we can help you with making the contacts."

"And the last option?" I asked.

"To terminate the pregnancy," she said.

"Yes, tell me about how the abortion works. I heard there is a pill that you take and that takes care of it." I said.

She spent the next few minutes going through everything. Since I may be at ten weeks already and was clear with her that I needed at least a few days to figure it out, Cheryl said that the doctors would give me some pills to take that would start the process, but that I would still need to come in for a procedure, a surgery kind of thing.

It was like I was back in school, watching an informational video, sitting at my desk, just watching. Kind of paying attention, kind of not. It didn't matter.

Except now it did.

SEVENTY-SEVEN

Jess

I know you're not supposed to, but I did anyway. Cheryl talked to me about not drinking, especially early in the pregnancy, but I didn't really want to think about it.

The bar was busy, the dance floor filled. A lot of Downies pressing together, holding their Bud Light bottles up in the air.

A group of guys were jammed together at a couple of round tables under one of the big screens, on a golf trip from up north. Jersey or Philadelphia. It really didn't matter where they were from and I didn't care. They drank shots of tequila—good stuff, too, not that lousy Cuervo crap. After a while, they started with the usual guy shit with Macy and me. Asking us to come back to their place later for a party, go swimming in the pool at the big house they were renting. Of course, we didn't say that we wouldn't, both doing our best to keep them there, drinking and tipping for as long as possible. At one point, they got together two hundred-dollar bills, offering one to each of us if Macy and I would do body shots off the other. Having done that for free more than once since we worked together, I laid her back on the bar, dripped in a little Jack and slurped it up slowly, with my tongue, the guys cheering and high fiving each other.

When I was done, we switched spots, the men all gathered in more closely around us, gawking and panting, hard-ons across the board I was sure. A vodka drinker, Macy pulled my tank top up exposing the bottoms of my breasts, and poured a perfect line of Grey Goose Orange from the middle of my chest down and into my belly button. She hopped up on the bar, straddling me, her ass up in the air, in downward dog yoga position. In one long endless lick, she polished off the vodka. We happily grabbed our hundred dollar bills, hugged the guys like they were our best friends, and went into the back.

Bobby was in the kitchen, leaning against the dishwasher.

"We done yet?" he said.

"That ought to do it, yep," I said, holding up the bill.

We went back out and Bobby rang the bell for last call.

After a round of shots on the house, Bobby's idea, the golfers paid their tabs, and went outside to wait for their cabs or Uber rides. A few grabbed my ass. A couple others stared, trying to get me to respond with some deep and meaningful eye contact, hiding their wedding rings in their pockets. I just smiled, told them how much fun they were, and that we hoped they would come back.

"Good tippers, those golfers," Macy laughed, slapping me a high five.

SEVENTY-EIGHT

Jess

I woke up the next morning not remembering much of anything.

"I've got to head out, Jess. Got work to do here, some water problem with the apartment next door," Bobby said.

I felt nauseated. The drinking. Being pregnant. One or the other. Possibly both.

Bobby set a Starbucks and some aspirin down on the table, sitting down on the bed. "You were in classic form last night," he said.

I looked under the covers. Nothing on. I looked back up at him, not saying anything, tongue still glued to the roof of my mouth.

"Don't remember? Fun time was had by all," he said, smiling.

I nodded my head, ringing now.

"Just kidding. You were pretty cooked by the time we got home. I got you out of your clothes and put you in bed. Stayed just to be sure you didn't puke all over yourself," he said.

"That was nice, thanks," I slurred.

He leaned his head away. "Might want to brush those teeth. Get yourself a shower, a little sleep. See you in a couple of hours at The Wreck," he said.

"Yep, okay," was all I could muster.

Once I heard the door close, I ran into the bathroom, banging my hip into the sink on my way to the toilet, head down, throwing up again.

* * *

My neck stiff from a short nap, head on the toilet seat, I pushed myself up and got into the shower, hot water running on me until it ran icy cold, clearing the fog.

I jumped back into bed, sipped the coffee, the cobwebs shaking off some. Looking over at my dresser, the pictures of me and my dad and now, a new one, of all of us—the four of us—I just could not believe it. All I had done, all I had been through been through over the last year and here I was, same place as my mom was all those years ago. Both my moms. Young. Finally, a whole life to be lived. One that was happy and fun and what I wanted. A boyfriend. Someone who loved me. Hard as it was for me to believe. Loved. Me.

I had that traction Jamie talked to me about during all of those therapy sessions over the years. *"Just get some traction, Jess. Do something to move forward. Then things will get better,"* I remember her saying.

But now, fuck, now I had this to deal with. Pregnant. Seriously? Not only did I not have any idea what I should do, but also I had no idea how to even figure out what I should do. I did know that I had to decide. Soon.

My mom made the sane, rational decision, it seemed to me. She was young, too young, and did what was right for her. She got married to the man she loved, they built a family together. She certainly didn't count on me and all my bullshit when she made that family but it was still hers. Her family.

What about Karen? She wasted a year of her life, gave her babies away. But she did give us a life. Granted, that life sucked a lot of the time, but there were good parts too. My dad. Pops. Macy. And now, my life—my life—it's better. Better because of a decision she made.

My mom, Lianne, she had a life but she could have had another one. What would hers have been like without me? Better?

What about Bobby? Do I tell him? Should I ask Macy what to do?

My brain was pop, pop, popping away. Like a printer that keeps going even when you push all the buttons to make it stop.

And, what about this baby? If I keep her, how will I raise her?

Will I love her or hate her for wrecking my life? It's taken me twenty-three years to just get to where I am. How can I do all of this with a baby?

But how could I end her life? Easy enough for me, but what about after? I don't know how I could live with it. And adoption, I just don't know. If she were like me, all fucked up, uncontrollable and impulsive, how would her parents do? Would they still love her?

I have to do something. Decide. But how?

* * *

I finished my coffee and set the cup back down.

I picked up my phone and made a call.

SEVENTY-NINE

JB

I was back. Not back in the office, although certainly I was. I mean back. Enjoying myself, talking to clients, joking with others in the hallway. Trying to catch a quick view up Pam's skirt when she was on the phone, legs stretched out behind the reception desk.

"Some mail for you," Pam said, dropping it in front of me.

As usual, Pam opened most of the mail before it made its way to my desk, scanning each piece into the appropriate client directory. The usual lawyer's mail, I thought to myself, sifting through a set of interrogatories in the Vaughn case, a deposition notice from that little yutz lawyer down the street, Rich Kimble, a scheduling order in a new case and one nasty-gram from opposing counsel in another notifying me of my client's irrepressibly bad behavior.

A few months ago, I couldn't have done it. Looking at the pile of paper, much less wading through it, would have sent me for a walk downstairs, out of the building and down the street, to nowhere in particular. Just out. Anywhere.

"Thought you might want to open this one yourself," Pam said, handing me an envelope. It felt like a card. The envelope had been addressed to me by hand, not computer generated like most of the cards I get, mostly around the holidays from vendors or other lawyers telling me about their decision to donate to a particularly wonderful cause instead of spending the money and sending around cookies or wine or some other package of shit that is either given away or finds its place in the garbage.

I looked over at Pam. She stayed at my desk, waiting.

"You might want to step out, in case it explodes when I rip it open," I said.

"Don't get too many cards around here," she said. "I want to see."

It didn't blow up.

The card was blue and gray, stripes on the bottom and some kind of design at the top. In the middle, there was a square, like a small board, that read:

"Sometimes, the people we count on the most are the ones who hear 'thank you' the least."

The "thank you" was underlined in pen.

I opened the card to see the rest, which said, *"Since you're one of those people, I hope you always know how much you are appreciated."*

The card came from a client, Paige Fender, whose case settled late last year after a lot of litigation that went on just as she was in the midst of chemotherapy treatments for advanced stage breast cancer.

Paige had also written a lengthy note inside the card, in the same pen used to underline "thank you" on the front. She mentioned my hard work in the case and said, *"I am still lost so much of the time, but am doing my best to climb out of the hole, and get on with this life. I guess life is short and we all search for peace, love, and happiness."*

It came up on me fast. I handed the card to Pam and sat down, spinning in my chair away from her and toward the window. Only clients cry in my office.

"How the fuck about that," I whispered.

"Yeah, how the fuck about that, Bro," Pam said.

* * *

After a few minutes, my iPhone rang.

"Jess Porter" popped up on the display.

"Hey, Jess," I said. "Good to hear from you. How you doing?"

"Hi, Uncle Bro," she said.

Quiet.

"Jess, what's up?"

"Uncle Bro, I need your help."

A Note from the Author

I want to thank my good friend Allison Kraemer for sharing her adoption story with me.

A necessary thanks also to Julie, my lifelong love and partner in all that is inappropriate. I could not have done it without you.

My first novel, *Card Game*, was a book I thought about for years. It was a book I wanted to write.

In life, we often are called on to do things we have to do.

Such was the case with this novel.

-DB

Roundfire

FICTION

Put simply, we publish great stories. Whether it's literary or popular, a gentle tale or a pulsating thriller, the connecting theme in all Roundfire fiction titles is that once you pick them up you won't want to put them down.
If you have enjoyed this book, why not tell other readers by posting a review on your preferred book site. Recent bestsellers from Roundfire are:

The Bookseller's Sonnets
Andi Rosenthal

The Bookseller's Sonnets intertwines three love stories with a tale of religious identity and mystery spanning five hundred years and three countries.
Paperback: 978-1-84694-342-3 ebook: 978-184694-626-4

Birds of the Nile
An Egyptian Adventure
N.E. David

Ex-diplomat Michael Blake wanted a quiet birding trip up the Nile – he wasn't expecting a revolution.
Paperback: 978-1-78279-158-4 ebook: 978-1-78279-157-7

Blood Profit$
The Lithium Conspiracy
J. Victor Tomaszek, James N. Patrick, Sr

The blood of the many for the profits of the few... *Blood Profit$*
will take you into the cigar-smoke-filled room where American
policy and laws are really made.
Paperback: 978-1-78279-483-7 ebook: 978-1-78279-277-2

The Burden
A Family Saga
N.E. David

Frank will do anything to keep his mother and father apart. But
he's carrying baggage – and it might just weigh him down...
Paperback: 978-1-78279-936-8 ebook: 978-1-78279-937-5

The Cause
Roderick Vincent

The second American Revolution will be a fire lit from an
internal spark.
Paperback: 978-1-78279-763-0 ebook: 978-1-78279-762-3

Don't Drink and Fly
The Story of Bernice O'Hanlon Part One
Cathie Devitt

Bernice is a witch living in Glasgow. She loses her way in her
life and wanders off the beaten track looking for the garden of
enlightenment.
Paperback: 978-1-78279-016-7 ebook: 978-1-78279-015-0

Gag
Melissa Unger

One rainy afternoon in a Brooklyn diner, Peter Howland
punctures an egg with his fork. Repulsed, Peter pushes the plate
away and never eats again.
Paperback: 978-1-78279-564-3 ebook: 978-1-78279-563-6

The Master Yeshua
The Undiscovered Gospel of Joseph
Joyce Luck

Jesus is not who you think he is. The year is 75 CE. Joseph ben
Jude is frail and ailing, but he has a prophecy to fulfil...
Paperback: 978-1-78279-974-0 ebook: 978-1-78279-975-7

On the Far Side, There's a Boy
Paula Coston

Martine Haslett, a thirty-something 1980s woman, plays hard on
the fringes of the London drag club scene until one night which
prompts her to sign up to a charity. She writes to a young Sri
Lankan boy, with consequences far and long.
Paperback: 978-1-78279-574-2 ebook: 978-1-78279-573-5

Tuareg
Alberto Vazquez-Figueroa

With over 5 million copies sold worldwide, *Tuareg* is a
classic adventure story from best-selling author
Alberto Vazquez-Figueroa, about honour, revenge and a
clash of cultures.
Paperback: 978-1-84694-192-4